Ivanhoe

THE BLACK KNIGHT

IVANHOE

Sir Walter Scott

Adapted by William Kottmeyer
Director, Reading Clinic
St. Louis Public Schools

Illustrations by William Hopkins

Webster Publishing Company

St. Louis   Atlanta   Dallas   Los Angeles

The Everyreader Library

Ivanhoe

Cases of Sherlock Holmes

The Gold Bug, and Other Stories

A Tale of Two Cities

Simon Bolivar

Other Titles in Preparation

Contents

Chapter 1

WHERE was King Richard of England? His work in the Holy Land was done. He had led the Christians in war against the Turks. At last the Turks had agreed to let the Christians come to Jerusalem. They could visit the holy city of Jesus Christ. England's king had fought like a lion in battle. He feared nothing. Fair-haired, blue-eyed Richard the Lion Hearted was Europe's hero. On his way home he had been taken prisoner. The Duke of Austria, his bitter enemy, had caught him alone. But the whispers were spreading through England.

"Richard is on his way!"

"The Lion Hearted is coming!"

"Soon we Saxons will get our rights back."

The rich Norman nobles were getting their soldiers together again. They took away the lands of the Saxon princes. They made slaves of the poor Saxons.

Two of these Saxons were resting on a rock in a forest. The older one wore a leather jacket. His rough sandals were tied with strips of leather. Around his waist was a broad leather belt. From the belt hung a horn. A long wicked knife was stuck in the belt. His beard and hair were a dirty yellow. Around his neck was a brass ring like a dog's collar. On the ring were these words: *Gurth, slave of Cedric of Rotherwood.*

Near him sat a younger, strange looking fellow. He wore a bright purple jacket. Over this he wore a red cloak. He had thin silver bracelets on his arms. He wore the same kind of brass collar. On his collar was cut *Wamba, slave of Cedric of Rotherwood.* One stocking was red, the other yellow. He wore a tall, pointed cap. Small bells hung from the point. The bells and the silly look on his face told what he was. The rich people in those days kept a clown, or fool, in their homes. These fools were to keep them laughing and amused at home. Wamba was one of these.

"A curse on those pigs," cried Gurth, the swine herder. He blew his horn. His pigs were eating the forest acorns. They did not come. "Somebody is going to get one of those pigs! Here, Fangs! Fangs!" he called to his wolfish dog. "Wamba, you've got to help me. If I don't bring those pigs—"

"I've just asked my legs about it," said Wamba. "They say no. They think it's unfriendly to carry me in that mud. Call Fangs back. You may as well let those pigs go. They'll be in Norman bellies anyway."

"That's the truth, Wamba. The Normans take the best of everything. There aren't many Saxons to stop them. God bless our master, Cedric. He's doing what he can. He'll go down fighting. But Reginald Front-de-Boeuf is coming back here. That'll be the end of Cedric. Here, here!" he called. "So ho, so ho! That's it, Fangs! You've got them. You've got them. Bring them on."

"Gurth, you'd better not let Front-de-Boeuf hear you. You're only a poor swine herder. But you'd be hanging on one of those trees. You'd better shut up about the Normans."

"Wamba, you dog! You wouldn't tell on me!"

"No, I'm only a clown. But—listen! Who is coming?"

They heard the sound of horses.

"Never mind," said Gurth. He had got his pigs together. Now he began driving them ahead of him. "Listen to that thunder! The rain is coming. Let's get home. This will be a terrible night."

Chapter II

THE horsemen soon overtook the two. One was a priest. He was fat and wore fine clothes. His sleeves were lined with rich furs. A beautiful gold pin held his cloak together. His servant rode near him. Two other priests rode a few yards behind him.

The other man was about forty years old. He was tall and strong. He had the look of a soldier. His face was burned almost black by the sun. His eyes were dark and sharp. A deep scar ran along his forehead.

He wore a long red cloak. On the right shoulder was a white cross. Under the cloak was an armor shirt. His gloves were metal. He rode a great strong horse. He was saving his war horse for fighting. His squire led the riderless war horse. On the saddle hung a short battle ax. There was also a great metal helmet with plumes. A long sword clanked on the other side. A second squire walked beside the horse carrying his master's lance. He also carried his shield which was covered with red cloth.

4

Two dark Arabian servants rode behind the squires. They wore silver collars and bracelets. Their long crooked sabers were covered with gold. All rode fine Arabian horses.

Wamba and Gurth stared at the handsome riders. They knew the priest. He was the Prior, or head, of the Jorvaulx Abbey nearby. He was well known as a hunter and a man who loved a good time. He went around with the Norman nobles a great deal.

"My friends," called the Prior, "do you know the people around here? Where can we spend the night?"

"Why," said Wamba, "there is an abbey a few miles away. You could go there. An old hermit lives down that road. You could stay in his hut tonight."

The Prior shook his head. "My honest friend," he said, "those bells must have made you dizzy. We priests do not stay with other priests. We like to have the common people care for us. That gives them a chance to do good. Then God will reward them."

"Well, I may be a fool," said Wamba. "If you priests want to do good, you could help one another. Even a fool can see that."

"Shut up," said the Prior's friend. "Try to be more careful what you say. How do you get to——

5

6

what's the fellow's name, Prior Aymer?"

"Cedric," answered the Prior. "Cedric the Saxon. Tell me, my good fellow, are we near his home? Can you show us the road?"

"The road is hard to find," said Gurth. "And Cedric and his family go to bed early."

"That's about enough from you," said the rider. "They can get up, can't they? We're not asking or begging. We're telling them what we want."

"I don't know if I should tell you," said Gurth. "My master doesn't like visitors."

"Are you going to argue with me, you slave?" The rider came forward.

Gurth's hand went down to his knife. But Prior Aymer rode between the two.

"Now, Brian," said the Prior, "you must not hurt him. You're in England now. You're too used to killing Turks. Come, good fellow," he said to Wamba, "tell us the way to Cedric the Saxon's."

Wamba finally gave them some directions. He mixed them up so they could never find the house.

"Ha!" said Gurth. "They'll never get there if they follow your directions. That was smart, Wamba. You're not such a fool after all."

"It's just as well. I'd just as soon they wouldn't see the Lady Rowena. There might be trouble.

Cedric might get into a fight with them. And Cedric can't fight all the Normans."

By now the riders were far ahead.

"I wish you hadn't stopped me," said the man called Brian. "I would have beat some sense into that Saxon's head."

"It wouldn't have helped us any," answered the Prior. "And it would make Cedric angry. Remember what I told you. This Cedric is proud and jealous. He's not afraid even of his Norman neighbors, Reginald Front-de-Boeuf and Philip de Malvoisin. He's a bull-headed Saxon. And he's proud of it."

"How can he have such a beautiful daughter?"

"He isn't her father. He is related to her. She comes from higher blood than he. He is her guardian. Don't think she isn't a beauty! Wait till you see her."

"She'd better be pretty. You remember our little bet? You bet me she's as pretty as any girl I've ever seen."

"I haven't forgotten. I bet my gold collar against ten kegs of wine. The wine is as good as mine now."

"Ha, ha! You mean your collar is in danger."

"Now listen to me, Brian. Be a little more polite than you are. I don't want you to fight with this Cedric. And be careful how you look at Rowena.

He loves her like a daughter. Why, he threw his own son out of the house! The son got to liking Rowena too much to suit Cedric."

"All right, all right. I'll be careful. But don't think any Saxon can throw me out of his house. I'm staying."

"Well, here are the two roads. The clown said to take the left one."

"No, he didn't. He said the right."

"I'm sure it was left."

They argued for a while. Then Brian saw some-one lying near the road.

"Here is someone, sleeping or dead," he said. "Let's ask him. Squire, jab him with my lance."

The man jumped up.

"Well," he cried, "what do you want?"

"We are lost," said the Prior. "Do you know these parts? Where is Cedric the Saxon's home? Do you know?"

"I'm going there myself," said the stranger. 'If I had a horse, I'd show you the way. The place is hard to find."

"We'll lend you a horse. Here, get up," said the Prior.

The stranger got on the horse and started off. The others followed. He seemed to know where he was going. At last he stopped.

"There," he said pointing. "There is Cedric's house." He pointed to a large, low building. "That's Rotherwood."

"Fine," said the Prior. "By the way, my friend, who are you, anyway?"

"Just a pilgrim," answered the stranger. "I've just come back from the Holy Land."

"Why didn't you stay and fight the Turks?" asked Brian.

"Why didn't you, Sir Knight? I see by your white cross you are a Knight Templar. The Knights Templar said they'd take the Holy Land."

Brian made a move to go after the stranger. Again the Prior got in his way.

"How do you know this country so well, stranger?" asked the Prior.

"I used to live around here," he answered.

A deep moat, or ditch, ran around the house. A great fence stood inside the moat. On the west side was a big drawbridge. This drawbridge could be let down over the moat. The Templar reached for his horn. He put it to his lips and blew loudly. The rain began to come down hard.

Chapter III

IN the great Rotherwood hall the servants were getting Cedric's evening meal ready. Two great oak tables stood in the hall. There was a big fireplace at each end. Swords and spears and shields hung on the walls.

About one quarter of the hall was a step higher than the rest. Here sat the family and any important visitors. On this platform the table ran crossways. A rich red cloth covered it. The servants' table was set against it to form a big T. This servants' table was long and rough. Big oak chairs and benches stood on the platform. Long rough benches were at the lower table for the servants to sit on.

Two chairs at the upper table were higher than the rest. These were for the master and mistress. Cedric the Saxon was sitting in one. He looked angry. Cedric was hungry and he did not like to wait.

Cedric's face looked as if he had a nasty temper. He had great, broad shoulders. His face was broad.

His eyes were large and blue. You could see he was a proud and jealous man. His long yellow hair hung to his shoulder. He had few gray hairs, although he was almost sixty years old.

Cedric was not only hungry. He was worried. The Lady Rowena had gone to church. She had got back late. She was then changing her clothes. There was no news of Gurth. Cedric had sent him out after the swine. The Saxon land owners put a lot of their money into buying pigs. They let them feed out in the forests. It was easy to lose them. Cedric wished Gurth would get back soon. He liked to have Wamba near him, too.

"Where the devil is Gurth?" he shouted. "He's always been a good servant. Now he's out fooling around when I want him."

A servant said the time was only an hour after the curfew bell. The curfew was the signal to blow out the lights and get into the house.

"The devil take the curfew bell!" cried Cedric. "The Normans started that, too. Turn out the lights! That's so the Norman robbers can steal safely. Reginald Front-de-Boeuf and Philip de Malvoisin know what the curfew is for! I'll hear they've stolen the swine and killed my servant. And Wamba! Where is Wamba? They'll take him, too. Another fool for a Norman lord. We're all fools. We're

12

fools to stand for the Norman thieves! I'll fight every last one of them. Ah, Wilfred, Wilfred, my son! If you were only here. But, no, you had to leave your father in his old age."

Just then came the blast of Brian's horn outside the gate. The dogs howled and barked.

"Get to the gate," yelled Cedric. "See who is there. Bad news, I know."

A boy came running in.

"It is Prior Aymer of Jorvaulx, master. The good knight Brian de Bois-Guilbert, commander of the Knights Templar, is with him. They and their men ask to stay for the night. They're on the way to the big tournament at Ashby."

"Aymer? Prior Aymer? Brian de Bois-Guilbert?" said Cedric. "Both Normans! Well, I can't help it. My home is open to all travelers. Go. Take six servants. Let them take the strangers to rooms. Look after their horses and mules. Give them what they need."

Some of the servants ran out to obey.

"The Prior Aymer," said Cedric, "and the Templar. What did you say the Templar's name is?"

"Brian de Bois-Guilbert."

"Bois-Guilbert? I've heard much about him. Both good and bad. They say he is a brave fighter. They say he's proud and cruel. Well, it's only for

13

the night. Go, get out the best wine. You, girl, go to Lady Rowena. Tell her she need not come to the hall to eat—unless she especially wants to."

"Oh, master," said the girl, "she will want to come. She wants news of the Holy Land."

Cedric looked at the girl angrily.

"The Holy Land," said Cedric. "I, too, should want news. But, no. My son has disobeyed me. He is no longer my son. I will not think of him."

He hung his head. The doors at the end of the hall opened. The servants came in carrying torches. Behind them marched the guests.

Chapter IV

PRIOR AYMER had changed his clothes. Now he wore even more handsome clothing. The Templar, too, had taken off his armor shirt. He wore one of dark purple silk. He had taken off his hat. He had short, thick, raven-black hair. The Templar was a strikingly handsome man.

Behind the Prior and the Templar came the Pilgrim. His cloak of coarse black cloth covered his whole body. He wore coarse sandals. The broad brim of his hat hid his face. He carried a long staff in his hand. The Pilgrim saw that the servants' benches were pretty well filled. He sat down near the big fireplace and began to dry out his clothes.

Cedric got up to welcome his guests.

"Please excuse me," he said. "I speak Saxon. If you can speak it, please do. If you cannot, I can understand Norman enough to get by."

The Templar's eyes flashed. "I speak Norman French. That is the language of King Richard and his nobles. I can understand Saxon, if you want to speak it."

Cedric looked at him angrily. He said nothing more, though. He led his guests to two chairs. They sat down. Cedric called for the food. The servants carried it in.

Gurth and Wamba came in and took their places. Cedric growled at them, but was glad they had come back in safely. He turned to his guests.

"Our food is plain here," he said. "But there is enough. Eat and be welcome."

There was plenty of good food. Just as they were about to begin, a servant at the door called:

"Stop! Place for the Lady Rowena."

A side door opened and Rowena came in. Behind her were four of her ladies. Cedric looked surprised and a little angry. He jumped up, though, and took her by the arm. He led her to her place at his right. All stood up. She sat down at her place. Now all the others sat down again.

The Templar whispered to the Prior.

"You keep your gold collar. You win the wine. She *is* a beauty!"

"I told you so," said the Prior. "But watch yourself. Cedric sees you."

But Brian did not listen. He kept staring at the Saxon beauty. Rowena was tall and fair. She had clear blue eyes. Her golden-brown hair was braided with jewels. Her dress was sea-green silk. A silk and gold veil lay on her shoulders.

Rowena saw Brian staring. She quietly pulled the veil over her face. Cedric saw what she did.

"Sir Templar," he said, "we do not stare at our Saxon ladies here."

"I'm sorry," Brian said to Rowena. "I didn't mean to bother you. I beg your pardon." He looked at Cedric. "I beg nobody else's pardon, though."

"The Lady Rowena will forgive us, I am sure," said the Prior. "May we see her at the tournament?"

"I don't know if we'll go," said Cedric.

"I hope you will," said the Prior. "The roads are dangerous. Brian could see that you got there safely."

"Sir Prior," said Cedric, "I need no help. I have my sword. I have my men. If we go to Ashby, my noble friend Athelstane will go along. No robbers would dare stop us."

"Sir Knight," said Rowena to Brian, "do you have news from the Holy Land?"

"Not much, lady," said Brian. "The fighting has stopped. Christians may visit the Holy City."

Rowena started to ask more, but stopped. Just then the gate keeper came in.

"There is a stranger at the door, master. He begs to come in."

"Let him in," said Cedric. "The night is bad. Give him what he needs."

Chapter V

OSWALD, Cedric's servant, came back. He whispered into Cedric's ear:

"It is a Jew. He calls himself Isaac of York."

"The Lord help us!" cried the Prior. "An unbelieving Jew! You will not let him into the same room with us, Cedric?"

"A dog Jew!" said the Templar. "I fought in the Holy Land. Shall he come near me?"

"This is my house," said Cedric. "Any traveler gets food and a bed here. I can turn no one away."

Into the hall now came a tall, thin old man. He bowed to left and right. He had keen black eyes under a high forehead. He was frightened and showed it. He wore a long cloak and a high square yellow cap. He took off his cap and looked for a place at the lower table. The Saxon servants did not move. They did not even look at him.

Cedric did not see him come in. The Pilgrim did see him, though. Isaac now stood helplessly still. The Pilgrim walked over to him. He took him to his own chair near the fireplace.

"Old man," he said, "my clothes are dry. I have eaten. You are wet and hungry. Sit here." He got the old man some food. Then he walked to the other end of the hall.

Cedric was talking with his guests.

"Now tell us," said Cedric to the Templar, "who did the best fighting in the Holy Land?"

"Well, I should not answer that. I am a leader of the Knights Templar. The Templars led the fighting."

"How about the Knights of St. John?" asked the Prior. "My brother fought with them."

"They fought well," said the Templar, "but—"

"Were there no great fighters from King Richard's army?" asked Lady Rowena.

"Forgive me, lady," said Brian. "King Richard did bring good fighters. They were second only to the Templars."

"Second to NONE!" said the Pilgrim. He had been listening to the talk. All turned to look at him.

"I say they were second to NONE," he said again. "I saw the big tournament after the battles. I saw King Richard and five of his knights take on all comers. I saw them each fight and throw down three men. And seven of them were Knights Templar. Seven Knights Templar were rolled in the dust. Brian de Bois-Guilbert knows that's true."

Brian's face twisted in rage. His dark face got even darker. His hand shook. His fingers crawled to his sword. Cedric was happy to hear this news.

"I'll give you this gold bracelet, Pilgrim," he shouted, "if you can tell me the English knights' names!"

"I'll do that. King Richard himself won first place."

"Good."

"The Earl of Leicester was one knight. Sir Thomas Multon was another."

"Ah, Multon is a Saxon."

"Sir Foulk Doilly and Sir Edwin Turneham were two others."

"Both Saxons! And who was the other?"

The Pilgrim was quiet for a minute.

"The sixth one was a young, unknown knight. I forget his name," he said at last.

"Sir Pilgrim," sneered Brian. "You haven't forgotten his name. I'll tell his name. It was the Knight of Ivanhoe. And I'll say this. If he were in England I would fight him again. Yes, and this time I would beat him. I hope he will be at the Ashby tournament."

"He would fight you today if he were here," answered the Pilgrim. "If Ivanhoe comes back from the Holy Land, he will fight you. I promise you that."

"You promise! Who are you? How can we believe you?"

"I need not say anything," said the Lady Rowena. "But I know Ivanhoe will meet anyone."

Cedric could say nothing. First a look of joy and pride came over his face. Then he closed his mouth tight, and frowned.

"Lady," he said, "this is no woman's business. I, too, promise Ivanhoe will meet this knight."

A little later all went to their bedrooms. The Templar passed old Isaac.

"Unbelieving dog," he said, "are you going to Ashby?"

"I hope to."

"To try to squeeze out a little more gold. You must have plenty on you now."

"None! Not a penny! Not one penny! I go to borrow money from my friends."

"Liar!" said the Templar. He went on to bed.

Chapter VI

THE servant Oswald led the Pilgrim to his room. Oswald whispered:

"Would you like to come to my room, Sir Pilgrim? We servants would like to have news from the Holy Land. We all love the Knight of Ivanhoe. We have heard little since he left."

"I have told what I know, boy. I leave early. Show me to my bed."

Oswald frowned and called a boy with a torch.

"This Pilgrim is not friendly to Christians. Take him next to the Jew's room. Good night, Pilgrim. Thanks for nothing."

"Good night," said the Pilgrim calmly. "God bless you."

A few steps farther Lady Rowena's maid stopped him.

"Pilgrim, the Lady Rowena wishes to speak to you. Follow me."

The Pilgrim followed. The maid opened the door to Lady Rowena's rooms. The rooms were richly furnished.

Lady Rowena was sitting in a big chair. The Pilgrim came forward and bowed.

"Pilgrim," said the lady, "tonight you spoke a name. I mean the name of Ivanhoe. All should be glad to hear it here. And yet, only I dare ask. Where did you leave him?"

"I know little about him," said the Pilgrim. "I am sorry. I wish I could tell you more. He had enemies in the Holy Land. But he overcame them. He will soon be back in England."

"I wish he were here," said Rowena. "I wish he would fight in the tournament at Ashby. If Athelstane wins the first prize, there will be bad news for Ivanhoe."

The Pilgrim said nothing.

"How did he look, stranger?"

"He was darker and thinner than when he went over with Richard. He seemed worried and sad."

23

Then Lady Rowena handed him a piece of gold. The Pilgrim took it, bowed, and left.

In his cold little room, the Pilgrim put out the torch. He threw himself on the hard bed and slept. When the first sunbeams came through the tiny window, he awoke. He got up and spoke his prayers. Then he went to the next room.

Isaac the Jew lay there, talking in his sleep. "God of Abraham!" he mumbled. "Spare an unhappy old man! I am poor. I haven't got a penny—"

"Don't be afraid, Isaac. I come as your friend. Quick! Get up. You'd better get out fast. You are in danger." Isaac was wide awake now.

"Holy Pilgrim!" said Isaac. "Why do you help me?"

"Don't worry about that. Last night the Templar spoke in Turkish to his servants. I understand the language. He told them to watch and follow you. When you get away from the house, they're going to catch you. They are going to take you to the castle of Philip de Malvoisin or Reginald Front-de-Boeuf."

Isaac grew pale with fear. He began to shake. He sat back on the bed.

"What shall I do?"

"Stand up, Isaac, and listen!" the Pilgrim said. "I'm going to help you. We shall leave now. The others are still asleep. I know a secret path through the forest. I'll show you the way. You can get safely to Ashby."

"Oh, thank you, Pilgrim. You are kind. I haven't got a penny, believe me."

"I don't care if you have or not. Why should I harm you? So long as I am a Pilgrim, I take no money. Stay here if you want. Cedric the Saxon may take care of you."

"He will not let a Jew travel with him," said Isaac. "And the road to Ashby goes through the lands of Philip de Malvoisin and Reginald Front-de-Boeuf. Good Pilgrim, I will go with you. Let us hurry. Come."

"Wait. I must get someone to let us out."

He led the way into the next room. Gurth lay snoring on the bed.

"Get up, Gurth," he said. "Open the back gate. Let the Jew and me out."

"What? The Jew is leaving? And going with the Pilgrim?" As he spoke, Wamba came in. Gurth lay down again.

"You can wait till they open the big front gate," he said.

"You will do this for me, Gurth," said the Pilgrim. He leaned forward and whispered something in his ear. Gurth leaped to his feet.

25

"Just open the gate," said the Pilgrim. "You shall know more later."

Gurth ran to obey him. Wamba and the Jew followed. Both wondered at the sudden change in Gurth.

"My mule, my mule!" said the Jew when they were outside.

"Get him his mule," said the Pilgrim. "Get one for me, too. I'll go with him. And, Gurth, listen to me. This is what I want you to do—" Now the Pilgrim whispered something in Gurth's ear.

"It shall be done," said Gurth. And off he went.

Soon they saw Gurth coming with the mules. The travelers crossed the narrow moat bridge to meet him. The Jew quickly tied something to the saddle. It was a small blue leather bag. He covered it with his cloak. "Just some clothes," he said nervously.

The Pilgrim got on his mule. He held out his hand to Gurth. The swine herder bent his head and kissed it.

The two travelers rode steadily through the forest. At last the Pilgrim stopped.

"See that big old oak tree?" he said pointing. "That marks the end of Front-de-Boeuf's land. We are long past the lands of Malvoisin. You now have nothing to fear. We are not far from Sheffield. There you will be safe."

"Blessings on you, good Pilgrim," said the Jew. "I have friends in Sheffield."

"Good," said the Pilgrim. "We will part at Sheffield, then.'

"Wait, wait," said Isaac. "I want to do something for you. God knows I am poor. I am no more than a beggar. They have robbed me. My goods, my money, my ships are gone. Still, I know what you need. I can get it for you. Right now you need a horse and armor."

The Pilgrim looked up, surprised.

"How did you guess that?" he asked.

"No matter," smiled Isaac. "I guessed it and I can get what you need."

"But I wear a Pilgrim's cloak. I am a holy man."

"Well, you said a few things last night that gave you away. And I saw something under your cloak. You carry a knight's gold chain and gold spurs. They shone when you stooped over my bed this morning."

The Pilgrim smiled. "Suppose I searched you, Isaac, as your eyes have searched me. What would I find?"

"Nothing, nothing," said Isaac quickly. "I have nothing." He took out a piece of paper and began to write. When he had finished he gave it to the Pilgrim. "In the town of Leicester all men know

27

the rich Jew Kirjath. Give him this paper. He has six fine harnesses for sale. He has ten good war horses. He will let you pick what you want. You may have anything you need for the tournament. When it is over, you give it all back—unless you can pay for it."

"But, Isaac," smiled the Pilgrim. "Do you know tournament rules? The loser's armor and horse go to the winner. Maybe I'll lose."

The Jew looked worried. But he answered quickly, "No—no—no—you will win. The blessing of Our Father will be on you. Your lance will be strong as the rod of Moses."

"Thank you, Isaac," said the Pilgrim, again smiling. They parted and took different roads to Sheffield.

Chapter VII

TIMES were not good in England. King Richard was the prisoner of the cruel Duke of Austria. No one knew where he was held. Prince John, Richard's brother, ruled the country. When Richard came back, John would rule no longer. So John did everything he could to get the Duke of Austria to hold Richard. Richard had always been good to John. But John loved power. He cared nothing for his own brother. He was weak and vain and selfish. He gathered the Norman nobles to his side. The Normans knew Richard would handle them roughly. They were glad enough to keep John in power.

The English people had their troubles. They could forget them at the tournaments. Everybody loved to see the tournaments. They could see the best knights in the country fight one another. The tournaments were always exciting. Old and young came in great crowds.

The tournament at Ashby was to be a good one. Some of the best knights were to fight. Prince John himself was coming. Rich and poor people had been pouring into Ashby for days.

Ashby was a fine place for a tournament. Not far from town was a great forest. At the edge of the forest lay a big meadow. On the other side of the meadow was a row of oak trees. The meadow sloped down to a flat center. A fence ran around the flat center land. It was about a quarter of a mile long and half as wide. At each end were great gates. Here were the heralds, or announcers, and the trumpets. A group of soldiers were here also to keep order. Near the south gate was a platform. On the platform were five pavilions which looked like little houses. The five pavilions were for the five challenging knights. Before each pavilion hung the knight's shield. Pennants with the knight's colors flew from the roofs. The knight's servant, or squire, stood before the pavilion. They had given the middle pavilion to Brian de Bois-Guilbert.

Along the fences were the seats. They were covered with carpets and cushions. Here sat the nobles and their ladies. The poor people had to stand. Hundreds had already climbed into the trees to watch.

One block of seats was higher than the others. Here were the finest carpets and cushions. Here, too, was a throne. Squires, pages, and other servants waited at this place of honor. Prince John and his nobles were to sit here.

Straight across was another block of seats. Here sat a row of pages and girls. Another throne had been built here. Above the throne flew the pennants. These pennants had pictures of hearts and bows and arrows. On the throne was a sign: The Queen of Beauty and Love. No one knew who the Queen would be.

Knights and nobles slowly filled the seats. The

great and rich ones sat in the upper seats. The less important people sat lower. Several fights soon started about these seats.

"Dog of an unbeliever!" said an old man. "Do you dare touch a Christian and a Norman gentleman?"

He said this to the Jew, Isaac of York. Isaac was richly and beautifully dressed. He was pushing his way to a seat. With him was his daughter, Rebecca. All eyes turned to the beautiful Jewess. She hung on to her father's arm. Her eyes were wide with fright. But Isaac knew he was safe here. Many nobles wanted to borrow money. They would help Isaac. Even Prince John was then trying to borrow some money from the Jews of York.

So Isaac pushed the Norman again. Some of the other Normans now got angry. Isaac might have been in trouble, but just then the people began to shout. Prince John and his nobles had ridden through the gate. With him were several Knights Templar. They came riding past the seats.

Prince John's quick eye saw what was wrong. He knew Isaac well. But now he stared at Rebecca. He had never seen her before. Rebecca was as beautiful as anyone he had ever seen. She had dark, shining eyes and smooth black eyebrows. Her teeth were white as pearls. The lovely black hair lay thick on her neck. Her dress was of richest Persian silk. Not one of the noble ladies could match her.

"By the bald scalp of Abraham," said Prince John, "there is a beautiful woman. What do you say, Prior Aymer? Have you ever seen better? I say the Jew and his daughter shall have a seat. Ho, Isaac! Is she your wife or daughter? Who is that Eastern beauty?"

"My daughter Rebecca, your Grace." He bowed low.

"You shall have seats. Who is sitting up there? Saxons! Fat, lazy Saxons! Move over there! Make room for my money lender and his lovely daughter."

Prince John was speaking to Cedric and his family. With him was his friend Athelstane. Athelstane was a great ox of a man. He stared dumbly as if he had not heard. John looked at him angrily.

"That big Saxon pig must be asleep. Stick him with your lance, De Bracy," he called to a knight near him.

De Bracy obeyed orders. He swung his lance around at Athelstane. Before he could touch him Cedric leaped up. He whipped out his short sword. He swung like lightning. With one blow he clipped off the point of De Bracy's lance.

The blood rushed into Prince John's face. He swore. But the crowd yelled and clapped. John

looked around angrily. He spied a young man in Lincoln green laughing and shouting.

"What are you shouting about?" asked John.

"I always shout when I see a good shot or a good blow," he said calmly.

"Is that so?" sneered Prince John. "You must be a good shot yourslf."

"Pretty good." The young man was not frightened at all.

"Keep your eye on him," said John to his men. "We'll tend to him later. We'll see how good he is."

"I'll be here," said the stranger.

John turned back to the seats.

"Now, you Saxon dogs. Move! I said the Jew shall have his seat."

"No, your Grace!" begged Isaac. "It is not right for me to sit there."

"Get up there, unbeliever. I told you to."

Isaac began to climb up to the seats.

"Let me see someone stop him," said John looking at Cedric. Cedric looked as if he were going to throw Isaac out. Just then Wamba began his clowning. Everyone burst into a laugh. Prince John threw back his head and laughed, too.

"Here, Isaac," he called. "Lend me some coins."

Isaac fumbled in his money bag. Prince John reached over and took the bag away. He threw a handful of coins at Wamba and rode on. The crowd laughed and clapped. Isaac crept to a seat with Rebecca.

Chapter VIII

AS the nobles rode forward, Prince John suddenly turned to the Prior.

"Prior, we have not picked the Queen of Love and Beauty. She is to give the prize to the winning knight. I give my vote to the black-eyed Rebecca."

"Holy Virgin!" answered the Prior. "A Jewess! I swear she is not so lovely as the Saxon Rowena."

"Saxon or Jew," said the Prince. "What's the difference? I say Rebecca. That would shame those Saxon louts."

"No, no," said De Bracy. "Let's let today's tournament winner pick the queen."

"If Brian wins I know who will be queen," said the Prior.

"Come," said another noble, "let us sit down. It's time the tournament started."

Knights began to gather at the north gate. These were to fight the five great challengers. Soon the gate opened and the first five rode in. From behind the pavilions, the music began to play. All eyes were on the five knights. They rode forward to the challenger's pavilions. Each one could pick the man he wanted to fight. He would ride up and touch his lance to the man's shield. They could fight with blunt or sharp lances. If the knight touched the shield with the lance handle, they would use blunt lances. If he used the point, they used sharp lances.

Each man touched a shield with his lance handle. Now they rode back up to the gate. They turned around and lined up. They held their lances up and ready. Brian's men now mounted their horses and lined up against them. With Brian were Reginald Front-de-Boeuf, Malvoisin, and two others.

The trumpets blew. The knights rushed at each other at full speed. Brian and three of his knights crashed their men to the ground. The fifth man got a draw. Both he and his enemy broke their lances. The trumpets blew again. The crowd cheered the winners.

A second and a third group of five knights came out. Not once were Brian and his men unhorsed. Then only three knights rode out. They would not touch the shields of Brian or Front-de-Boeuf. But the other three challengers again won.

The crowd grumbled. Malvoisin and Front-de-Boeuf were not well liked. The other three challengers were strangers. Cedric the Saxon was not pleased at all. The challengers were Normans. He looked at Athelstane.

"The fight is against England, my friend," he said. "Will you not try your luck?"

"I fight tomorrow," answered Athelstane. And nothing Cedric said would change his mind.

Suddenly there came the clear sound of a trumpet. All eyes turned to the north gate. Who was the new champion? The gate flew open and in he rode!

The new fighter was of middle size. He was slender and graceful. His steel armor was inlaid with gold. On his shield was a young oak tree, pulled up by the roots. Under it was the Spanish word *Desdichado,* or "Disinherited." He rode a gallant black horse. When he passed Prince John he saluted with his lance. He rode his horse so well, the crowd cheered.

"Touch Ralph de Vipont's shield. He's the easiest," they called.

The new champion rode on. Up to the pavilions he rode. To the crowd's surprise he struck the shield of—Brian de Bois-Guilbert! He gave it a sharp ringing blow with the *point* of his lance.

"Are you ready to die, brother?" asked the Templar.

"Are you?" asked the strange knight.

"Take your place. Get a last look at the sun. Tonight you will sleep in heaven."

"Thank you," said the Disinherited Knight. "You'd better get a fresh horse and a new lance. You're going to need them."

Now he backed his horse skillfully all the way to the gate. There he stood waiting. Brian did take a new shield. He also got a fresh, strong horse and a new tough lance.

The two champions stood facing each other. The crowd held its breath. Few thought the Disinherited Knight could hold his own.

The trumpets blew. The champions flew from their places. They crashed together in the center like thunder. Both lances broke into splinters. The horses reared high on their hind legs. Both riders dug in their spurs. They looked angrily at each other, turned, and rode back. The crowd was roaring. Their squires gave each a new lance. Then all became quiet.

The knights rested for a few minutes. Prince John again gave the signal. The trumpets sounded. Again the riders thundered at each other.

This time the Templar aimed at his enemy's

shield. He hit it squarely. His lance broke into pieces. The Disinherited Knight was almost thrown. He aimed his lance at the Templar's shield. But he changed his aim at the last second. He swung his lance up to the helmet. The helmet was much harder to hit. Fair and true he hit the Norman. His lance held in the steel bars. The Templar's saddle straps broke. Saddle, horse, and man rolled in a cloud of dust.

The Templar broke loose and jumped to his feet. Angry at losing, he pulled out his sword. He waved it at his enemy.

The Disinherited Knight leaped from his horse. He pulled out his sword. He ran back to meet the Templar. But the others rode between them. The tournament rules would not let them fight with swords.

"We shall meet again, I hope," said the Templar. "Then no one will stop us."

"On foot or horseback, with spear, ax, or sword. Any time, any place," answered the Disinherited Knight.

The Disinherited Knight now told a herald to blow his trumpet. He was going to take on the others in any order.

Big Front-de-Boeuf was the first.

The trumpets sounded again. The two knights

40

charged. Both broke their lances. Front-de-Boeuf broke his stirrup in the crash. The judges ruled the Disinherited Knight the winner.

He won again in the third fight. He caught Philip Malvoisin's helmet on his lance point. The helmet laces burst open. The helmet tore off, saving Malvoisin a bad fall.

The fourth knight's horse pulled away as they charged. The Disinherited Knight held up his lance and let the helpless knight go by. He rode back to give him another chance. But the knight gave up.

Ralph de Vipont was the last. The Disinherited Knight hurled him to the ground on the first charge. He landed with a crash. The blood gushed from his nose and mouth. They carried him senseless from the field.

The Prince and the judges had the heralds call out the winner's name. The people shouted and cheered. The day's honors could go only to the Disinherited Knight.

Chapter IX

THE tournament judges were the first to shake the winner's hand. They tried to get him to take off his helmet. The Disinherited Knight would not take it off. He could not let his face be seen, he said. There was no rule about it, so the judges let him keep it on.

Prince John was not pleased. He wanted to know who the winner was. Also, he was angry because Brian had not won. He turned to his nobles.

"Can any of you guess who he is?" he asked.

"I cannot guess," said De Bracy. "I don't know a knight who can beat five good men in one day. I'll never forget how De Vipont hit the ground. I thought lightning hit him."

"Maybe he's one of the knights who went with King Richard to the Holy Land," said another.

"It may be the Earl of Salisbury."

"It may be Sir Thomas de Multon."

"It might—it might be Richard the Lion Hearted himself."

Prince John got pale. He looked around nervously.

"God forbid!" he cried. "Remember you men promised to stand by me."

"Don't worry about that," said De Bracy. "It's not Richard. You know Richard couldn't squeeze into that armor. That knight is three inches shorter than Richard. Richard's shoulders are about twice as broad."

By now the judges had brought the winner to John's throne. John spoke to him. The Disinherited Knight said nothing. He bowed low. The judges brought in the prize. It was a big fine war horse.

"Sir Disinherited Knight," said John, "there is something you must do. You must name the fair lady who will be Queen of Love and Beauty. Raise your lance."

The Knight obeyed. Prince John put a gold crown on the lance. Now the knight rode slowly past the crowd. At last he stopped where the Lady Rowena sat. The champion slowly lowered his lance. He laid the gold crown at Rowena's feet. The trumpets sounded. The heralds called her name.

Some of the Norman ladies grumbled. The people, though, shouted, "Long live the Lady Rowena, Queen of Love and Beauty!" Prince John now rode to Rowena.

"Put on your crown, fair lady. Tonight we have

a great dinner at Ashby Castle. We hope you and your family will come."

Rowena was silent. Cedric the Saxon rose and spoke for her.

"The Lady Rowena does not speak Norman French. Athelstane and I speak only Saxon. We thank Your Highness. We cannot come to the dinner. The Lady Rowena will be here, though, tomorrow."

Cedric put the crown on Rowena's head.

John and his nobles now rode away. As they were leaving, John saw the young man in Lincoln green. He pointed him out to his knights.

"Don't let that fellow get away."

The young man looked straight into John's eyes.

"I'll not leave Ashby until day after tomorrow. I shall shoot in the bow and arrow contest," he said.

"He'd better be good," said John to his men. "If he isn't, he'll pay for it."

The crowds now moved toward Ashby. Many nobles were staying at Ashby Castle. The knights who had fought rode back together. As they rode they talked over the day's fighting. Soon many little fires were started in Ashby. The armor makers were getting to work. Broken armor had to be repaired for the next day's fighting.

Chapter X

THE Disinherited Knight's squire stuck his head into the tent.

"Five squires are here," he said. "They want to talk to you."

The Knight had on a long robe and a hood. The hood hid his face, so he stepped out boldly. The five knights whom he had beaten had sent their squires. Each squire led his master's war horse. On the horse was the knight's armor. They were obeying tournament rules. In a tournament, the loser had to give the winner his horse and armor. The winner could take money instead, if he wanted to. Usually he took the money. The money was called "ransom" for the horse and armor.

The first squire spoke.

"I come from Brian de Bois-Guilbert. Here are his horse and armor. You may keep them or ask ransom."

The other four said about the same thing. The Disinherited Knight spoke to the other four first.

"I give you four the same answer. I shall not take the horses and armor. I would like to take nothing at all. I have nothing myself, though. I'll take a small ransom."

"We each offer a hundred gold coins for the horses and armor."

"Enough. I'll take half of that. Split one quarter among yourselves. Give the other quarter to the heralds and tournament servants."

The squires thanked him. The Disinherited Knight now spoke to Brian's squire.

"I'll take nothing from your master. We will fight to the death some day. He is no friend of mine. Take his horse and armor back. If he won't take them, keep them yourself."

The Templar's squire bowed and left.

"Well, Gurth," said the Disinherited Knight to his squire, "I did well with them."

"I'm doing pretty well, too," said Gurth. "I'm a Saxon pig chaser. How am I playing a Norman squire?"

"I've been afraid someone would recognize you."

"Tush!" said Gurth. "Only Wamba would know me."

"Here's your share, Gurth. Ten pieces of gold."

Gurth put them in his pocket. "I'm the richest swine herder in the world," he said.

"Take this bag of gold to Ashby," said his master. "Find Isaac the Jew of York. He lent me the money for my horse and armor. Pay him."

Isaac and Rebecca were staying at the home of a rich Jew near Ashby. Rebecca was sitting in a big chair. Isaac was walking back and forth.

"Oh, father," said she, "forget about losing the bag of gold. Prince John took it. You couldn't help it."

"It hurts, though, daughter. And I will lose the money I lent to the Disinherited Knight. I was foolish. A Christian won't pay back a Jew unless the law makes him."

A servant came in. He whispered to Isaac that a Christian wanted to see him.

"Bring him in," he said. "Rebecca, put on your veil."

Gurth came in. "Are you Isaac of York?" he asked.

"I am."

"I come from the Disinherited Knight. He sends you the money for his armor. The horse is back in your stable. How much for the armor?"

"I knew he was a good, honest lad! How much money have you?"

"Not much," answered Gurth.

"You've got a hundred coins in that bag. It's a heavy one. How about making it eighty gold pieces? Even then I won't make a penny on the deal."

"Seventy is enough."

"No, no. Eighty. Pay me."

At last Gurth gave in. He counted out the eighty coins. Isaac looked at the bag.

"You have more there."

Gurth grinned. "About eighty more," he said. "Too bad you didn't ask for them." He walked out.

Rebecca had gone out before him. When Gurth walked down the stairs she was waiting for him.

"How much did you pay my father?" she asked.

"Eighty gold coins."

"Take this purse. It holds a hundred gold coins. Give eighty to your master. Keep the rest yourself."

"This is no Jewess," said Gurth. "This is an angel from heaven!"

Chapter XI

THE crowd began to gather early. On this second day of the tournament the knights would make up two teams at once. The Disinherited Knight led one team. The other was led by Brian de Bois-Guilbert. Each side had about fifty knights ready to fight.

Athelstane was among the fighters. He had joined Brian's team. Cedric was angry about it. He hated the Normans, and Brian was a Norman. Athelstane would not tell him why he wanted to fight with the Norman knights. The truth was simple. Athelstane was jealous. He had long wanted to marry Rowena. Cedric wanted him to marry her, too. But Rowena had other ideas. She had liked Cedric's son, Wilfred, very much. Wilfred liked her. When Cedric found that out, he had had a fight with Wilfred. Cedric had told Wilfred to get out. Athelstane had hoped Rowena would marry him when Wilfred left England with King Richard. Now this unknown knight had picked Rowena as Queen of Love and Beauty. Athelstane wanted a chance to shame him before Rowena's eyes.

When Rowena took her seat, the music started. The noble ladies crowded around her throne. Brian and his fifty knights lined up at one end of the field. The Disinherited Knight and his fifty men were at the other end. The sun shone on the bright lances and armor. The heralds called out the rules for the fighting. Prince John gave the signal. The trumpets blew. The lances were lowered. The knights dug their spurs into their horses.

49

They rushed upon each other. They met in the center with a shock heard a mile away. Great clouds of dust arose. When the dust settled, the crowd gasped. Half the knights had been pitched from their horses. Some were on their feet. These were fighting hand to hand. The wounded were mopping up blood with their scarves. The mounted men with broken lances were swinging their swords.

The Disinherited Knight and Bois-Guilbert tried to get to each other. Both were still on their horses. Both had broken their lances. They went at it with their swords. Both were skillful swordsmen. The crowd roared to see them fight.

Big Front-de-Boeuf had been battering men down on one side of the field. The giant Athelstane, too, had cleared his side. Both spied the Disinherited Knight and Brian at once. Both had the same thought. Get the Disinherited Knight! Front-de-Boeuf spurred his horse forward. Athelstane came from the other side. They would have had him, but the crowd shouted, "Watch out! Watch out!"

The Disinherited Knight suddenly pulled his horse back. Athelstane and Front-de-Boeuf crashed together. They turned, and in a moment all three were upon the lone champion.

For a few minutes his horse saved him. He turned and dodged like a hawk. He was able to keep his enemies apart. First he darted at one, then at another. Again the people cheered him. But the end was near. He could not hold off the three.

Suddenly help came. Among the Disinherited Knight's men was a tall champion in black armor. He rode a large black horse. He had hardly fought at all. A few knights had attacked him, but he had calmly beaten them off.

Now he saw the three after the Disinherited Knight. He spurred his horse forward. He let out a shout and came on like the wind.

He was just in time. Front-de-Boeuf had his sword raised to swing. The Black Knight hit him like a falling tree. The blow smashed from the helmet down to the horse. Front-de-Boeuf and his horse went down. Both lay still.

Now the Black Knight turned to Athelstane. He had broken his sword on Front-de-Boeuf. He pulled the Saxon's battle ax out of his hand. One mighty clout and Athelstane lay senseless on the field.

The Black Knight now rode coolly away. The Disinherited Knight went after Brian. When the Disinherited Knight charged, his enemy's horse went down. Brian could not pull his foot from the stirrup. He lay helpless on the ground. The young champion jumped from his horse. He held his sword over the fallen man's head.

Prince John saved the Templar more shame. He suddenly gave the heralds the signal. The trumpets blew. The fight was over. So ended the tournament of Ashby.

Prince John now had to name the second day's champion.

"It shall be the Black Knight," he said.

His friends thought the Disinherited Knight should have the honor.

"He unhorsed six men," they argued. "And he won over the enemy leader."

"Brian's men would have won," said Prince John. "The Black Knight saved his side. He shall take the prize."

To everyone's surprise, the Black Knight could not be found. The heralds called twice for him. No one had seen him. John then had to name the Disinherited Knight champion again.

"Disinherited Knight," said John, "go to the Queen of Love and Beauty to be crowned champion."

The Disinherited Knight bowed.

Again the trumpets blew. The ladies waved their silk handkerchiefs. The people shouted. The judges led the champion to the Queen's throne.

He knelt before her. She reached down to put the golden crown on his helmet. The judges called, "No, no! His head must be bare." They came

53

forward and cut his helmet loose. They pulled it off. All saw the sunburned face of a young man of twenty-five. His face was pale as death and streaked with blood.

Rowena could not choke down a cry. Then, hands shaking, she put the beautiful crown on his blond head.

"I give you this crown, Sir Knight, as prize for the day's champion."

The Knight bent his head and kissed her hand. Slowly he sank lower and lower. Before anyone could help, he dropped flat at her feet. He had fainted.

Cedric was struck dumb. The Disinherited Knight was his own son, Wilfred of Ivanhoe! The judges picked him up and stripped off his armor. They soon saw why he had fainted. The head of a lance was buried in his side. They hurried him off the field to the hospital tent.

Chapter XII

"THE Disinherited Knight is Wilfred of Ivanhoe!"

"It is Cedric's son!"

"Wilfred is back from the Holy Land!"

Ivanhoe's name flew from mouth to mouth.

"I might have guessed it," said Prince John. "One of my brother Richard's men!"

Waldemar Fitzurse went over to look at Wilfred. Soon he came back.

"You won't have to worry about him for a while. He is badly wounded. The Lady Rowena almost fainted herself when she saw him."

"Who is this Lady Rowena?" asked Prince John.

"A very rich Saxon princess," said Prior Aymer. "She's a rose of beauty and a jewel of wealth."

"We'll cheer her up," said Prince John. "We'll marry her to a Norman. What do you say, De Bracy? Would you like to marry her and have her lands?"

"If the lands are good, I'll take the bride," said De Bracy.

"I'll not forget it. Ask the Saxons to come to the dinner tonight."

Just then a servant came running. He put a letter into John's hands.

"From whom?" asked John.

"France," said the servant. "A Frenchman brought it. He said he'd ridden night and day to get it here."

The Prince looked at the seal. It was from his friend, the King of France. John opened it nervously. He read the words:

"Watch yourself. The Devil is unchained."

John was pale as death. After a minute he took Waldemar Fitzurse and De Bracy aside. He showed them the letter.

"You know what it means. My brother Richard has got loose."

"Well," said Fitzurse, "let's get our men together. A few days may be too late. Let's cut this tournament short."

"The common people want the shooting contest," said John. "Let's not get them angry."

"It's not late," said Waldemar. "Let's have the shooting right now instead of tomorrow."

"That's a good idea, Waldemar," said John. "I'd like to pay back that loud fellow in Lincoln green. We'll have the dinner tonight, too."

The heralds called for the shooting contest. The

winner was to get a silver horn and a silk belt. The men began to gather. John spied the man in Lincoln green.

"Well," said John, "aren't you going to shoot?"

"I'm not afraid to shoot."

"What is your name, anyway?"

"Locksley."

"Then, Locksley, if you win the prize I'll add twenty gold pieces. If you lose, we'll take that Lincoln green suit. Then you'll get a good whipping with bowstrings. How's that?"

They put the target up at one end of the field. The men took their places. One by one they took their shots. Ten out of twenty-four arrows landed on the target. Two of the ten were in the inner ring. Hubert, one of Malvoisin's forest rangers, had put them there. The judges named Hubert the winner.

"Now, Locksley," said Prince John, "will you shoot it out with Hubert?"

"All right. I'll shoot two shots at this target with Hubert. Then Hubert ought to shoot at my target."

"That's fair," said John. "Hubert, beat this fellow and I'll fill the horn with silver."

"I'll do my best. My grandfather shot a bow at the battle of Hastings. I shoot as he did."

A fresh target was now put up. Hubert shot first.

He aimed long and carefully. The arrow whistled through the air. It hit the inner circle, but was not quite in the center.

"You forgot about the wind, Hubert," said Locksley.

As he spoke, Locksley stepped up carelessly. He did not even aim. The arrow thumped into the very center of the target. Prince John ground his teeth.

"Hubert, are you going to let him beat you?"

"I'll do my best. But my grandfather shot a—"

"The devil take your grandfather!" shouted John. "Shoot! And shoot your best."

Hubert took his place again. This time he hit the very center of the target.

"Good shot!" called the crowd.

"You can't beat that, Locksley," sneered Prince John.

"No, but I can still split the arrow," said Locskley.

He let his arrow fly. It split Hubert's arrow apart. The crowd was so surprised they could say nothing.

"The Devil himself must be shooting," whispered one. "I never saw anything like it."

"Now," said Locksley, "let's shoot at my target."

He walked over to a willow tree. He pulled down a long, thin branch. Now he peeled off the bark.

"A man who can hit this at a hundred yards can shoot," said Locksley.

58

"My grandfather shot a bow in the battle of Hastings," said Hubert. "He never shot at anything like that. Neither will I. If he can hit that stick at a hundred yards, I give up. I'd rather shoot at a sunbeam."

"Cowardly dog," said Prince John.

The white stick was put in the ground a hundred yards away, Locksley bent his bow.

The arrow split the willow stick.

Even Prince John cheered.

"You've won the horn and the twenty gold pieces," he said. "I'll make it fifty if you join my men. You're the best shot I've ever seen."

"Pardon me, noble Prince," said Locksley. "I will serve no one but your brother Richard. The twenty gold pieces I give to Hubert."

With these words Locksley slipped away.

Chapter XIII

PRINCE JOHN had his dinner at Ashby Castle in fine style. He asked the Saxons Cedric, Athelstane, and others to come. John looked for trouble when Richard got back. He wanted to keep as many people on his side as he could.

Rowena would not come to the dinner. Athelstane and Cedric did come. John welcomed them politely. But when the Saxons sat down, the Norman nobles began to make sly fun of them. Athelstane was not quick enough to see this. Very little got by Cedric, though. As the evening went on he became more and more angry.

At last the dinner itself was over. The men kept on talking about the tournament and drinking. Prince John's thoughts were elsewhere. He could not hide his fears. Suddenly he rose and held up his drinking cup.

"We drink to the health of Wilfred of Ivanhoe," he called. "His wound keeps him away tonight.

Everyone drink in honor of Cedric, father of a good son."

"No, my lord," said Cedric, rising. "I will not call him my son. He has disobeyed me. He is no longer my son."

"You will not be angry at what I have done, then," said Prince John. "I have given the lands of Ivanhoe to Reginald Front-de-Boeuf. He is going to keep them."

"Yes, I'm going to keep them," shouted Front-de-Boeuf. "Call me a Saxon dog if Wilfred or Cedric takes them away!"

That was enough for Cedric.

"Who would call you a Saxon? You can't wipe a Saxon's boots. No Saxon would insult a guest as you have done."

"Front-de-Boeuf's tongue is too quick," said Prince John. "Here, I fill my cup to Cedric himself. We drink to your health, Cedric."

The Norman nobles pretended to drink.

"Now, sirs, that is fair to our Saxon guests. Cedric, will you now drink to a Norman? Then we will be true friends."

Cedric rose and filled his cup.

"Your Highness asks me to drink to a Norman. I will. I drink to the best and noblest of all Normans. I drink to the health of—Richard the Lion Hearted!"

There was dead quiet for a moment. Prince John had expected his own name to be spoken. He had his cup to his lips. When he heard his hated brother's name he set it down. Then he looked around to see what the others would do. One or two brave knights shouted, "Long live King Richard!" Some did what the Prince had done—put their cups back down. A few, like Front-de-Boeuf and Bois-Guilbert, did not touch their cups at all. Cedric looked around a minute. Then he said, "Up, Athelstane. Let's get out of here. These Normans can make fun of us some other time. We've got a long trip home. Let's start."

"Don't worry," whispered Fitzurse to Prince John. "De Bracy and I will keep the nobles in line."

"They're afraid," said John. "They know Richard is coming. They'll run like rats."

"I wish he weren't scared to death himself," whispered De Bracy to Fitzurse. "His brother's name starts him shivering."

Fitzurse did what he could do with the nobles. He tried to show them they had better stick with Prince John. Most of them agreed. They were to meet at York and crown Prince John king of England.

Late at night Fitzurse got back to Ashby Castle. He met De Bracy in the hall. De Bracy was dressed like a forest ranger.

"What are you up to, De Bracy?" asked Fitzurse. "Why haven't you been working on these nobles?"

"Oh, come now, Waldemar. You're just working for yourself. I know what you're after. You know what I want. If Prince John is king, you and I will rise. So we're for Prince John."

"Well, why those forester's clothes?"

De Bracy laughed. "I'm going to get myself a wife. I'm going to catch those Saxons on their way home. I'm going to carry off the lovely Rowena."

"Are you crazy, De Bracy? The Saxons are rich and strong. You can't get away with it."

"They won't know I'm in it. They'll think forest robbers have caught them. I've got spies out now. Tomorrow we'll take them. Then I show up. I save the fair lady. I take her to Front-de-Boeuf's castle. And, Waldemar, if she says yes or no, she marries Maurice De Bracy."

"A wonderful plan—bah!" sneered Fitzurse. "Who helped you think this up?"

"If you must know, it was Brian de Bois-Guilbert. He's going to help me. His men will be the forest robbers."

"What a fool!" said Fitzurse to himself. "I'm trying to make a king out of a coward. He must go chasing women! Well, that's what I've got to work with."

Chapter XIV

BY now the Saxon travelers were well on their way home. Cedric was angry. After the tournament he had sent his servants to look after Wilfred. But some men had carried the wounded knight away on a stretcher. Then Cedric got angry with his son all over again. He had hoped Rowena would marry Athelstane. Rowena said she would never marry Athelstane. So Cedric was angry with Rowena. After the tournament Gurth had come back. Gurth would not say where he had been. So Cedric was angry with Gurth. He tied his hands and feet and made him a prisoner.

As they went on, they suddenly heard cries for help. They rode through the thick trees toward the sound. Soon they came to a stretcher lying on the ground. Sitting next it was a young woman. An old man walked up and down, groaning.

The old man was Isaac of York. The young woman was Rebecca. The man on the stretcher was covered with blankets. Isaac told how he had hired a bodyguard of six men at Ashby. A wood-cutter had told them that forest robbers were just ahead. The bodyguard had taken mules and horses and had run off.

"Will you let us travel with you?" asked Isaac.

Cedric was willing to send two men with them.

"They can take you to the next town," he said. "Then they can catch up with us again."

Rebecca came up to Rowena.

"I do not ask a favor for myself," she said. "But there is someone very dear to you. For his sake take the sick man with you. You will be forever sorry if you do not."

"The man is old," Rowena said to Cedric. "The girl is young and beautiful. Their friend is sick and in danger. Our men can carry the stretcher. Let them go with us."

Cedric agreed.

No one was watching Gurth very closely. He called Wamba to him. He whispered in his ear. Wamba loosened the ropes. Gurth slipped quietly away into the forest.

The travelers now started again. They came to a small brook. When half of them were across they were attacked. A band of robbers came at them from front and rear. In a minute it was all over.

Both Cedric and Athelstane were very quickly

overpowered. Four or five men dragged Cedric from his horse. They jumped at Athelstane before he could grab his sword.

No one got away except Wamba. Wamba picked up a sword and fought like a lion. When four or five men went after him, he leaped from his horse. In a moment he was gone through the thick bushes. He kept running until he heard his name called.

"Wamba!"

He looked around.

"Gurth!"

"What's the matter?"

"They are prisoners!"

"Who?"

"Cedric, Athelstane, Rowena, and the others."

"Let's help them."

"How?"

"Let's keep near them. We may have a chance."

"All right. Come on."

Neither Wamba nor Gurth saw the stranger come near.

"Just a minute, friends."

Wamba and Gurth jumped. The stranger looked like one of the forest robbers. He was dressed in Lincoln green. A silver horn hung at his belt. The belt was made of silk. Wamba and Gurth stared. It was Locksley wearing the prizes he had won.

66

"Who is taking prisoners?" Locksley asked them.

"I don't know who they are," said Wamba. "They're dressed just like you. Go find out."

"I'll do just that. You two stay here. I'll be right back."

A few minutes later he was back.

"I think I know them," he said. "We three can do nothing against them. They won't hurt the prisoners yet. We've got a little time. Come with me. I have enough men to take care of them. Let's get them."

Chapter XV

WHILE Locksley was gathering his men, Brian and DeBracy's men kept going. At last they got near Front-de-Boeuf's castle.

"You'd better leave us now, DeBracy," said the Templar. "You want to come back and play hero, don't you?"

"I've changed my mind," said DeBracy. "I'll stay to talk to Rowena when they're safe in the castle."

"Don't you trust me, DeBracy? Are you afraid of me? I'm not going to steal her."

"You do what you please."

"All right. I'll tell you the truth. I don't want your blue-eyed beauty. I've got a better one."

"Aha! Not the fair Jewess?"

"Have you got anything to say about it?"

"No. I just thought you'd like her father's gold better."

"I'll have both!" answered Brian.

Before long they saw Front-de-Boeuf's castle. It was the old Saxon Castle Torquilstone. Front-de-Boeuf's father had taken it years before.

When Cedric saw it, he guessed everything.

"And I thought forest robbers had us!" he cried. "Front-de-Boeuf! Well, dogs, what do you want? My life or my money? Let the Lady Rowena go and you can have both."

Nobody answered him. DeBracy blew his horn three times. Front-de-Boeuf's men lowered the drawbridge. They rode in.

They threw Cedric and Athelstane into one room. Rowena they locked in another. Rebecca was taken to a tower room high in the castle. They threw Isaac into a dark dungeon.

Isaac looked around him. Rusty iron chains hung from the walls. A pile of bones lay in the corner.

Isaac heard steps on the stair. The bolts screamed and the hinges creaked. Reginald Front-de-Boeuf came in. Behind him were two Arabian slaves.

First he locked the door. He walked up to Isaac slowly. The Jew sat with his mouth open. As the giant came closer Isaac shrank back. The slaves laid down some weighing scales.

"Cursed dog, do you see these scales?"

Poor Isaac nodded.

"In these scales you will weigh me out a thousand silver pounds."

"Holy Abraham!" cried Isaac. "Who has that much?"

"If you don't, you're going to have a hard time."

"Have mercy, noble knight! I swear I haven't—"

"Shut up!"

He made a signal to the slaves. They took charcoal from their baskets. They dumped the charcoal under a large rusty grate. In a few minutes the fire was glowing.

"See those iron bars over the fire, Isaac? That is your bed. That or get me a thousand pounds of silver."

"No, no, no! You wouldn't do that! Nobody could be so cruel!"

"Don't make me laugh, Isaac. I have seen thousands die. Do you think I care about the screams of

one poor Jew? Take your choice. Will you pay?"

Isaac looked at the red hot bars. He shivered.

"I will pay! I must beg the money. I haven't got it. But I will get it for you. Will you let us all go, then?"

"You mean those Saxon pigs? They pay, too. When do I get the silver?"

"Let my daughter Rebecca go to York. She will send the silver back."

"Your daughter?" said Front-de-Boeuf. "I gave her to Sir Brian de Bois-Guilbert."

Isaac let loose a ringing scream. He threw himself on the ground. He wrapped his arms around Front-de-Boeuf's knees.

"Take all you want," he cried. "Take ten times more. Stab me. Cook me. Kill me. But spare my daughter!"

"Strip him, slaves!" r o a r e d Front-de-Boeuf. "Chain him to the bars!"

Suddenly they all heard the clear blast of a bugle. Loud voices called for Sir Reginald Front-de-Boeuf to come.

"I'll be back, dog," he snarled. He ran out to see what the trouble was.

71

Chapter XVI

A LITTLE before noon DeBracy came up to see his beautiful prisoner. He was carefully shaved and his long black hair was curled. He wore the best clothes he had.

He took off his velvet hat when he came into the room. He waved Rowena to a seat.

"If you are my jailer, Sir Knight," she said, "I will stand. What do you want?"

"My dear Rowena," said DeBracy smoothly, "I am really your prisoner. Your beauty has made me your slave."

"I do not even know you, sir," said Rowena.

"I'm sorry you don't know me," said DeBracy. "I'm sure you have heard of me, though. I have a good name as a brave soldier."

"Brave! To kidnap a few old men and helpless women?"

"You are not fair, Lady Rowena," said DeBracy. "I hurt no one. You are the one I wanted."

"I want nothing to do with you!"

"All right. You want plain talk. Here it is. You will not leave this castle until you marry me. You live with Cedric and his pigs. I can make you a great lady."

"I am a Saxon. I have lived with Cedric since I was a child. I like his home. When I leave, it won't be with you."

"Don't be foolish. You'll never marry Wilfred. I'll tell you more. Your hero Wilfred is here in this castle now. All I have to do is tell Front-de-Boeuf. You know what Front-de-Boeuf will do, don't you? He wants to keep the castle and lands of Ivanhoe."

"Wilfred here?" said Rowena. "That's a lie."

DeBracy looked at her. "Don't you really know? Don't you know the man on the stretcher was Wilfred of Ivanhoe?"

"What if he is here? Why should Front-de-Boeuf harm him?"

"Don't you know that, either? Front-de-Boeuf wants his castle and lands. He'll do anything to get them. But look, Rowena. You marry me and Wilfred is safe. Don't marry me and he dies."

"Save him, for heaven's sake!" cried Rowena.

"I can. I will. You marry me, and I take care of him. I promise."

"You can't be so low."

"Don't fool yourself. I know just what I want.

Ivanhoe lies wounded in this castle. Front-de-Boeuf loves land more than anything else. You think he won't kill him? One swing of his dagger! One cup of poison!"

Up to now Rowena had been brave. Now she burst into tears. DeBracy was almost sorry for her.

"I wish she wouldn't cry," he thought. "I wish I was as tough and hard as Reginald Front-de-Boeuf."

Then came the clear blast of the bugle. DeBracy leaped for the door to see what the trouble was.

Chapter XVII

WHILE this happened Rebecca waited in her room. Two soldiers had pushed her through the door. In the room sat a wild looking old woman. When Rebecca came in the old hag looked up.

"Out of here, old crow," said one of the men.

"Once you would not have dared to speak to me like that."

"Good Dame Urfried," said the other man, "don't waste our time. Get along out of here."

"A curse to you both! What evil are they up to now?" said the old hag. She looked at Rebecca. "Ah, that's easy to guess. Well, no one can hear you scream up here."

"Will they kill me?" asked Rebecca.

"Oh, no. They won't kill you. Look at me. Once I was as young and pretty as you are. Then Front-de-Boeuf's father stormed this castle. My father and my seven brothers fought to save it. The stairs ran with their blood. I became the slave of the father and this Reginald."

She left the room and locked the door behind her.

Rebecca looked at the room. There was just one window. Outside the window was a sort of porch, or balcony. Rebecca looked out eagerly. The balcony was high above the moat. There was no way to get down. She turned away sadly.

As she did, the door opened. A tall man dressed in Lincoln green came in. His cap covered the upper part of his face. He stood before Rebecca. She pulled off two fine bracelets and held them out.

"Take these," she said, "and for God's sake be good to my poor father and me."

"Fair flower," said the forest robber, "those pearls are beautiful. They are not so beautiful as your teeth. The diamonds shine. They cannot shine like your eyes. I don't want jewels, Rebecca. I want you."

75

"Take the ransom! You can buy anything with gold."

"I don't want gold."

"You are no forest robber," said Rebecca. "A robber would take the gold. A robber would not speak Norman French. You are a Norman."

"You're right. I'm no robber," said Brian de Bois-Guilbert. He pulled off his cap. "I won't take pearls and diamonds from you. I will put them on those beautiful arms."

"Why don't you take money? You are a Christian. I am a Jewess. Your church will not let you marry me. I cannot marry you."

"I can marry you and be forgiven. You can join my church."

"Stand back," said Rebecca. "Listen to me! I'll tell everybody what you have done. You will be the shame of the Templars."

"Join my church and all will be well. I'll make you a great lady."

"Your church? To marry you? You coward! You liar! I spit at you. You shall not touch me!"

As she spoke, she opened the window. She ran to the very edge of the balcony.

Bois-Guilbert was too surprised to stop her. He took a step forward.

"Stay where you are," Rebecca cried. "If you come

one more step nearer to me, I tell you, I'll jump."

The Templar stopped.

"Come down," he said. "I swear I will not hurt you."

"I will not trust you. Stay where you are."

"Come, Rebecca. Let's not fight."

"Don't move!"

"You need not fear me."

"Not now, I don't. I'm ready to jump."

"I'm not always hard and cruel, Rebecca. Rebecca, you must marry me. I will be a great man. One day we Templars will rule the world. I will be the leader. I want you to be with me."

"I am a Jewess. You are a Christian."

"What's the difference? That does not matter."

Now came the loud clear blast of the bugle. Like Front-de-Boeuf and DeBracy, Brian was alarmed.

"I'll be back, Rebecca. I want to talk to you again about this."

Brian de Bois-Guilbert ran to see what the trouble could be.

Chapter XVIII

THE Templar hurried down to the great hall of the castle. DeBracy was already there.

"Where is Front-de-Boeuf?" asked Brian. "Who is blowing that bugle?"

"He is working on the Jew," answered DeBracy. "Isaac's howls must have drowned the bugle sound."

Soon Front-de-Boeuf came to them. He carried a letter in his hand.

"Now we'll see what this cursed noise is all about," he said. "Here, Brian, you can read this. What does it say?"

"This must be a joke," said Bois-Guilbert.

"Joke?" said Front-de-Boeuf. "Read it."

"Wamba, Gurth, the Black Knight, Robert Locksley, and his men write this to Reginald Front-de-Boeuf:

"You and your friends have taken Cedric the Saxon prisoner. You have also taken Lady Rowena and Athelstane.

"You will set them free. We give you one

hour. If you do not, we will come in and get them."

The knights looked at each other in surprise. De-Bracy broke out laughing. Brian began to laugh, too. Front-de-Boeuf did not think it was funny at all.

"They've got Front-de-Boeuf scared," said De-Bracy. "A fool and a swine herder have scared him."

"Don't be a fool yourself, DeBracy," said Front-de-Boeuf. "These fellows have some men out there. They wouldn't dare do this if they didn't." One of the servants came by just then. "Here, fellow," called Front-de-Boeuf. "How many men are outside the castle?"

"There are at least two hundred, sir," he answered.

"There you are," said Front-de-Boeuf. "You two stirred this up. Fools!"

"Oh, come, now, friend," said DeBracy. "What's a band of lazy pig stickers?"

"Did you ever see them shoot their arrows?" asked Front-de-Boeuf.

"Oh, stop this silly talk," said Brian. "Let's take our men and wipe them out."

"This is not a band of Turks," said Front-de-Boeuf. "These are Englishmen. Wipe them out? How? My best men are at York with yours, DeBracy. We have about twenty in the castle. Those and Bois-Guilbert's men are all we have."

"Send for help from your neighbors," said the Templar.

"Help from where? Malvoisin and his men are in York, too. So are my other friends. I'd be there if it weren't for you two."

"Well, let's send somebody after our men, then," said DeBracy.

"Who can get by them? They'll watch every path. It won't work. Brian, you'll have to write an answer to the letter."

"I'd rather answer with my sword. You're the boss. What do you want me to write?"

"Let's play for a little more time."

At last they agreed on the letter. Brian wrote:

"Reginald Front-de-Boeuf does not take orders from slaves. Here is your answer: We will kill the prisoners before noon. If you have a priest with you, send him in. We will let him get the prisoners ready for death."

The letter was sent out to the forest. Wamba, Gurth, the Black Knight, and Locksley were waiting. More than two hundred men were spread out in the woods. More were coming in every minute.

The letter was handed to the Black Knight.

He read it.

"Kill the noble Cedric!" said Wamba. "Sir Knight, that cannot be right."

"So the letter says," the Black Knight answered.

"Then," said Gurth, "we'll take the castle."

"They're just trying to gain time," said Locksley. "They don't dare kill them."

"I wish one of us could get into that castle," said the Black Knight. "We ought to find out how many men they've got. I think we could take it if we knew. We've got our chance. Who can play priest? They'll let a priest into the castle. If one of us goes, we can find out how they stand."

"I'm only a fool," said Wamba. "I'm just fool enough to try it. Get me a long black robe and a hood."

Chapter XIX

WAMBA stood before the castle door of Front-de-Boeuf. The gate keeper scowled. "Who are you? What do you want?"

"Peace be with you. I am a poor priest of St. Francis. I have come to speak to the prisoners."

The gate keeper went to speak to Front-de-Boeuf.

"Send him up," said the master. "Who are you?"

"I am a poor priest of St. Francis," answered Wamba. "I was traveling through the forest. The outlaws grabbed me. They said you wanted me to pray with some prisoners here."

"That's right. How many men are out in the forest?"

"About five hundred."

"What!" said the Templar. He had just stepped into the hall. "That many? Front-de-Boeuf, let him carry a letter to DeBracy's men. Now, let's let him see the prisoners."

"All right," said Front-de-Boeuf. He sent a servant to take Wamba to Cedric and Athelstane.

Wamba knocked on Cedric's door.

"Come in," called Cedric. "What do you want?"

"To get you ready to die."

"No! They don't dare!"

"Oh, yes, they do."

"I am ready," said Athelstane. "They're not going to scare me."

"Wait a bit," said Wamba. "Don't you know me?"

"Wamba!"

"Yes, Wamba. I'm here to help you. You, master, take my robe and hood. I'll stay here in your place."

"Go, Cedric," said Athelstane. "You can get help. If you stay we won't have a chance."

"Have we got a chance for help from outside?"

"Yes," said Wamba. "There are five hundred good men out there. Good-bye, master. Be good to Gurth. I may never see you again."

The tears stood in Cedric's eyes. "I'll never forget you, Wamba. But I hope to get help. Maybe we can save you all — Rowena, Athelstane, and Wamba."

The two now changed clothes.

"Good-bye, Athelstane. Good-bye, Wamba," said Cedric. "I'll save you or come back and die with you."

"Good-bye, master," said Wamba.

Cedric started out. In the dark hall a woman stopped him.

"I pray you, father, stop. There is a wounded man in this castle. Please speak to him."

But old Urfried came out and pushed Rebecca aside.

"Come this way, father," said the hag. "I will show you the way out. Come with me. I want to talk to you. You, Jewess, go to the sick man's room. Watch him until I get back."

Chapter XX

URFRIED now took Cedric to a small room. "You are a Saxon, father. The sounds of my own language are sweet in my ears."

"I am a Saxon," answered Cedric. "But get me out of here."

"Stay a little while," said Urfried. "I shall not live much longer. I want to tell you my story before I die. Father, I was once free, happy, loved. Now I am a poor slave. The old hag you see was once the princess of Torquilstone!"

"What!" cried Cedric. "You the daughter of Torquil Wolfganger? He was my father's best friend!"

"Your father's best friend?" cried Urfried. "Then you are Cedric of Rotherwood! Why are you in these priest clothes?"

"Don't worry about that now. Why are you here? We thought you were long dead."

"All these years I have lived here—"

"Evil woman! Your father and brothers died

85

fighting the robber Normans. And you—you live with the Normans!"

"I know. But I live to get revenge."

"In all these years you haven't got revenge? Did you never have a dagger? A knife?"

"I know, Cedric. Yes, I should have done it long ago. But I promise you I'll die like a true Saxon. Listen! There are soldiers outside the castle. Hurry out and lead them. Watch the castle. When you see a red flag wave from the top tower, charge. The red flag will mean there is trouble inside. Go! Hurry! You do your part and I'll do mine."

Cedric wanted to ask other questions, but now they heard Front-de-Boeuf's voice.

"Where is that loafing priest? Ah, there you are. Follow me. I'll let you out the gate."

Front-de-Boeuf led Cedric to the gate.

"Sir Priest," he said, "you see that herd of Saxon pigs around the castle? Tell them we have many men here. Tell them anything. Just so they stay away for about twenty-four hours. Then, take this letter to Philip de Malvoisin's castle. Tell them to send it to York as fast as they can."

"Oh, yes, Sir Knight. I'll do just as you say."

"Come back after it is over. I'll pay you well."

As they parted Front-de-Boeuf put a gold coin into Cedric's hand.

"Remember, I'll beat the hide off you if you don't do as I say."

Front-de-Boeuf locked the gate and called his man.

"Ho! Giles, bring Cedric of Rotherwood to me. Bring the other pig, too—Athelstane."

They brought the prisoners down to Front-de-Boeuf. Wamba kept Cedric's cap over his face. Front-de-Boeuf sat down and took a long drink of wine.

"Well, my bold English friends," he said, "how do you like my castle? Remember how nasty you got at Prince John's dinner? Well, you'll pay for that. I'll hang you from the windows and let the crows eat your flesh. Speak up, you Saxon dogs! How much ransom do I get? You, the pig from Rotherwood, how much?"

"Not a penny for me," said Wamba. "I don't care if you hang me up. I've been dizzy since I was born."

"What!" shouted Front-de-Boeuf. "Who is this?" He knocked Cedric's cap from Wamba's head and pulled his collar open. He saw the metal slave collar around his neck.

"Giles! Servants! Dogs!" shouted the angry Norman. "What have you brought me here?"

Just then DeBracy came in.

"I can tell you," said he. "This is Cedric's clown."

"He'll hang with his master," said Front-de-Boeuf. "Go, get the right Cedric. Bring him here. Can't you tell the difference between the fool and master?"

"Say!" said DeBracy. "Don't you guess what happened? He got out in the priest's robe and hood!"

"The dog!" roared Front-de-Boeuf. "I myself opened the gate for him. You!" he said to Wamba. "You will pay for this. I'm going to tear your scalp off. Then I'm going to throw you from the roof. So you're a clown, are you? Laugh that off!"

"Come on," shouted DeBracy. "They'll be at us in a minute. Call the Templar. Let's get to the walls."

The Templar had been watching the enemy.

"Say!" he called. "These men have a leader who knows something. Watch how they crawl closer to the castle. They keep under cover. You can't get a shot at them! They have no flag. I'll bet a noble knight is leading them, though."

"I see him!" said DeBracy. "I see the shine of his armor. Look! See that tall man in the black armor? You know who he is, Front-de-Boeuf? The same one who knocked you senseless at Ashby!"

"Good," said Front-de-Boeuf. "Now I'll pay him back."

They all now went to the walls. The enemy was getting close. Surely they would attack soon.

Chapter XXI

WHEN Ivanhoe was carried to the hospital tent at Ashby, he had been badly wounded. Cedric's men had come too late. Rebecca had already asked Isaac to send for the wounded knight. His men carried Wilfred to the house just outside of Ashby.

Wilfred did not come to for a long time. Rebecca looked at his wound carefully. She put medicines on it and bandaged it. Rebecca was a good nurse. She had a secret Jewish medicine, wonderful for healing wounds. Wilfred was soon out of danger. Rebecca was sure he could travel with them.

Isaac wanted to leave him at Ashby.

"I will pay for his care," he said to Rebecca.

"But, father," she said, "he needs our secret medicine. We cannot let anyone else use it. They may find out how to make it."

"That's true," said Isaac.

"And, father," Rebecca said, "you have lent money to Prince John. You'd better have a good friend if Richard comes back. Ivanhoe is Richard's friend. Be good to him. Maybe he will help you."

"You're a smart girl, Rebecca. We'll take him along tomorrow."

That night Wilfred opened his eyes. He wondered where he was. A few minutes later Rebecca came in. A black servant followed her into the room. Ivanhoe thought he must be back in the Holy Land.

"Gentle lady," he said, "I pray you—"

Rebecca smiled.

"I am Rebecca, a Jewess. My father is Isaac of York. I shall take care of you. I have a medicine which will soon heal your wound. No Christian doctor could heal you for a month at least."

"How soon can you heal me?" asked Ivanhoe.

"In eight days if you do as I tell you."

"I will. I believe you. Where is Cedric the Saxon? Where is the Lady Rowena? Where is Prince John?"

"Prince John ended the tournament. He hurried off to York. Nobles and knights rode with him. People say he will make himself king."

"Oh, no, he won't! I'll fight for Richard. So will others."

"Be careful. Stay quiet or you won't fight at all."

"That's right," said Ivanhoe. "How about Gurth, my squire? Where is he?"

"Cedric was angry with him. I'm sure he will forgive him, though."

"I've brought bad luck to him. I brought bad luck to my king, Richard. I brought trouble for the Lady Rowena. Lady, you had better turn me out. I'll bring bad luck to you, too."

"No," smiled Rebecca. "You're hurt and weak. That's why you feel that way. Be cheerful! You will do great things for your king. Now, take this medicine. Then rest. We must leave tomorrow."

The medicine put Ivanhoe to sleep. In the morning Rebecca came again to see him. He had no fever. Her servants got him on the stretcher. They started off on the trip which ended in Front-de-Boeuf's castle.

Chapter XXII

NOW Rebecca found herself with Ivanhoe again in the castle. She was happy to be with him. Danger was all around them, but she did not care. He looked up as she came back into the room.

"Oh, it's you, Rebecca. I am worried. I have guessed where we are. I heard the soldiers talking. We are prisoners, aren't we? And we're in Front-de-Boeuf's castle?"

"Yes, you're right. Brian de Bois-Guilbert and Front-de-Boeuf lead the men in the castle. A band of men are all around the castle. They're trying to get in. I don't know who they are, though."

Now the noise in the castle got louder. Soldiers were moving to the castle walls. Shouts told the soldiers where to stand. The sounds of clanking armor and swords came to their ears.

"I wish I could drag myself to that window," Ivanhoe said to Rebecca. "There I could watch the battle. If only I had a bow and arrows! If only I could swing a battle ax! I lie here and do nothing!"

"Don't worry. I'll stand at the window and tell you what happens."

"No, no! They'll shoot at every window when they start. Rebecca! Don't do it. There's a big shield in that corner. Put the shield in the window and stand behind it."

Rebecca dragged the big shield to the window. Now she could look out and still be safe. There was a stone tower on the other side of the moat. Front-de-Boeuf's men were in the tower. They were going to try to hold this tower. Their enemies were gathering in the forest near by. Between the tower and the castle ran the moat. If Front-de-Boeuf's men lost the tower, they could get into the castle over the drawbridge. Then they could pull the drawbridge up and fight from the castle. Rebecca told Ivanhoe what was happening.

"The woods are full of men with bows and arrows. They're sticking pretty close to the trees."

"What flag do they carry?" asked Ivanhoe.

"I can see no flag at all," answered Rebecca.

"That's strange! Can you see their leader?"

"Yes. He's a knight in black armor. He's telling the men what to do. Here they come! They're coming forward! The first men carry big shields. The men behind them are bending their bows. They aim!"

Just then came the sound of the bugle. The Norman trumpets from the castle blew also. The soldiers on both sides began to shout. The arrows flew like hail.

"What do you see, Rebecca?" asked Ivanhoe.

"Arrows so thick I can see nothing else," answered Rebecca.

"Arrows won't take the castle. Look for the Black Knight. What is he doing?"

"I see him now!" Rebecca cried. "He leads his

men right under the tower! They're hacking at it with axes. They're getting in! They're getting in!" screamed Rebecca. "No! The Normans push them out! Front-de-Boeuf leads the Normans. I see him high above the others. Now they're back in. They're fighting hand to hand."

Rebecca turned from the window.

"Look again, Rebecca. Look again."

"God of Moses! Front-de-Boeuf and the Black Knight fight hand to hand! He is down! He is down!

"Who is down?" cried Ivanhoe. "For our dear Lady's sake, tell me."

"The Black Knight," said Rebecca. Then she shouted with joy. "But no! But no! He is up again! He fights as if he were twenty men. His sword is broken. He snatches up a battle ax. He charges Front-de-Boeuf. He hits him! Again! Again! Again! The giant stumbles! He's going down! He's falling!"

"Front-de-Boeuf?"

"Front-de-Boeuf! His men rush to get him. The Templar leads them. They've got him! They drag him inside the walls."

"The Black Knight's men are at the tower, aren't they?"

"They are. They're at the walls! Some put up

95

ladders. Some climb on others' shoulders. The Normans throw the ladders down. The Normans have the best of it now."

"Are the Black Knight's men giving up?"

"No!" shouted Rebecca. "The Black Knight himself is at the big tower gate. He has a great ax. Can't you hear it thunder against the gate? The Normans throw big stones down at him! Now they're throwing heavy logs! He doesn't stop. He's still swinging."

"By our Lady!" shouted Ivanhoe. He raised himself on his bed. "I thought there was only one man could fight like that!"

"The gate shakes! It crashes! They rush in. They've won the tower. Oh, they throw the Normans from the tower into the moat!"

"The bridge, Rebecca! Have they won the bridge?"

"No. The Templar kicked the planks into the moat."

"Ah, but they'll get it yet. They can't keep them out. The Black Knight will beat the whole castle down. Can you see him, Rebecca?"

"Yes. He is black as a raven. He rushes to the battle. His great ax lays the Normans left and right. They run to get away."

Ivanhoe lay back on his bed and smiled.

Chapter XXIII

FTER the Black Knight's men took the tower, the battle stopped for a while. DeBracy came down to the castle hall. There he met Brian de Bois-Guilbert.

"Where is Front-de-Boeuf?" asked DeBracy. "They tell me he's been killed."

"He's not dead—yet," said Brian. "But ten suits of armor wouldn't have saved him from that ax. How did the English fight on your side of the castle?"

"Like devils," answered DeBracy. "They got close to the walls. I think that outlaw Locksley was leading them. I'm glad I've got good armor. He hit me seven times with arrows."

"You kept them out, didn't you? We lost the tower on our side."

"That's bad. We just haven't got enough men. Front-de-Boeuf is dying, too. Brian, let's give up the prisoners."

"What? Give them up to a band of outlaws? Outlaws led by a swine herder and a clown?"

"All right. All right. Let's get back to the walls, then. I can die as well as you can."

"To the walls!" answered the Templar.

Front-de-Boeuf lay on his bed. He was badly hurt. He was afraid he was going to die. He began to think of all the dirty tricks he had played in his life. As he twisted in pain, he heard a voice.

"Think about your sins, Reginald Front-de-Boeuf. Fighting against your own king! Murder! Robbery! Who got Prince John to war against his brother?"

"Who are you?" asked Front-de-Boeuf. "Whoever you are, you lie! I did not start Prince John against Richard! Not I alone. There were fifty others. Do I have to take the blame for fifty? Ah, there you are! I see you now, you dirty old hag! Old Urfried!"

"Yes, Reginald Front-de-Boeuf! Old Urfried!"

"Ho! Giles! Brian! DeBracy! Grab this old witch and throw her from the roof!"

"Louder, Reginald! Louder! Call them again. Listen to those sounds. This is the end of the Front-de-Boeufs. The Saxons are at your walls. They're coming in. And, Reginald, do you see the smoke? Can you smell it? Remember the big piles of wood stored under this room?"

"Woman!" roared Front-de-Boeuf. "You haven't set fire to it? By heaven, you have. I smell it!"

"The flames are rising fast," said Urfried. "Do you know what I'm going to do now? No? I'm going up to the highest tower. I'm going to put up a red flag. Do you know why? It's a signal. It's to let the Saxons know they can get in now. Good-bye, Reginald Front-de-Boeuf!"

Urfried slammed the door. Front-de-Boeuf heard her lock and double lock the door behind her.

Chapter XXIV

AFTER the tower was taken, the Black Knight got busy. He had the men build a floating bridge, or long raft. He wanted to use the raft to cross the moat. As soon as the raft was finished, the Black Knight spoke.

"There's no use waiting longer, my friends. The sun is setting. I can't stay another day. Let's take that castle. We'll open the tower door and throw the raft into the moat. Follow me across and help me. I'm going to beat the castle door down. The others can keep those arrows flying. When the Normans come to the wall, pick them off. All right.

Men! Let's go! Open that door. Throw that raft out."

The men pushed the big door open. They threw down the raft. It made a slippery path for two men at a time. The Black Knight leaped out on it. Cedric followed closely. In a moment they were on the other side. The Black Knight began to thunder his ax against the door. The Normans threw down stones and wood at him. A part of an old drawbridge still hung over the door. This kept the stones from hitting the Black Knight and Cedric. But the men who followed were out in the open. Two dropped with arrows in their hearts. Two more fell into the moat. The others backed up. The Black Knight and Cedric were now alone at the castle door. Their friends kept the arrows flying to help them.

"Shame!" shouted DeBracy. "Are you going to let those two dogs stay there? Hack down that old drawbridge. It will fall on their heads."

Now the men in the tower saw the red flag go up. Locksley's men saw it first from their side.

"Come on, men!" shouted Locksley. "Charge! Must the Black Knight and Cedric do it all? See that red flag? It's the signal. We have friends inside. The castle is ours. One charge and we take it."

He pulled back his bowstring. He sent the arrow

into the heart of a Norman on the wall. Another Norman was hacking at the old drawbridge. Locksley's next arrow went through his helmet. The Norman came tumbling down into the moat with a great splash.

"Don't give up!" shouted DeBracy. "Give me that ax!" He snatched it up and leaped on the wall. He hit again and again with the ax. Three times Locksley hit him. Three times the arrow bounced off DeBracy's armor.

"It's a Spanish steel coat," said Locksley. "The arrows won't go through. Ho! Sir Knight! Cedric! Come back! Let the old drawbridge fall."

Neither Cedric nor the Black Knight heard him. DeBracy would surely have crushed them. But then the Templar came running to him.

"All is lost, DeBracy. The castle is burning."

"No!" shouted DeBracy.

"The other side is in flames. I can't stop it." Brian was still cool as ice.

"Saints of Paradise!" swore DeBracy. "What shall we do?"

"Lead your men downstairs. Push the big gate open. There are only two men down there. Throw them into the moat. Then use the raft. Get over to the tower. Let's take it back."

"Good! I'll do my share."

He got his men together quickly. They rushed down to the castle gate. They threw it open. But as it opened, the Black Knight was on them. He pushed them all back. The two front Normans went down like trees. The rest backed up before this terrible champion.

"Dogs!" yelled DeBracy. "Will you let two men beat you?"

"He's a devil," said a soldier backing away.

"The castle is burning, you fool! Out of the way! Let me fight him myself."

Maurice DeBracy fought well. The walls rang with their blows. DeBracy swung his sword. The Black Knight used his battle ax. At last the Black Knight swung from his heels. DeBracy blocked with his shield. But the blow was too strong. Ax and shield together crashed down on DeBracy's head. He went flat to the ground.

"Give up, DeBracy," said the Black Champion. He stooped over him and held a dagger to his helmet bars.

"I don't know who you are," said DeBracy. "I won't give up to a strange knight."

The Black Knight whispered something into De Bracy's ear.

"All right," said the Norman. "I give up. I'm your prisoner."

"Go to the tower. I'll take care of you later."

"I will. Wilfred of Ivanhoe is a wounded prisoner up there. He'll die unless he gets help."

"Wilfred of Ivanhoe! Show me his room!"

"Go right up those stairs."

The Black Knight jumped for the stairs. Cedric's men now came up and took DeBracy's men prisoners.

As the fire spread, Ivanhoe and Rebecca began to smell the smoke.

"The castle is burning!" Rebecca cried. "What can we do?"

"Run, Rebecca, and save your life," said Ivanhoe. "I am done for."

"I will not go," said Rebecca. "We will be saved or die together."

Now the door flew open. The Templar stumbled in. His armor was broken and bloody. His face was burned.

"Rebecca!" he cried. "There is one way to get out. Come, follow me!"

"I will not follow alone. Save my father. Save this wounded knight."

"A knight is not afraid to die, Rebecca—"

"I will die before I get help from you, then."

"You'll do what I say! You fooled me once. You won't do it twice."

The Templar picked her up and swung her over

his shoulder. He carried her screaming from the room. Ivanhoe thundered after him:

"Hound of the Temple! I'll have your heart's blood!"

His cries led the Black Knight into the room.

"I wouldn't have found you but for your cries," he said. "Come, Wilfred of Ivanhoe, I'll carry you out."

"Let me alone. Get that villain! Save the Lady Rowena! Save Cedric!"

"Later," said the Black Knight. He picked Ivanhoe up as if he were a baby. The other men carried him over the moat. The Black Knight rushed back to save the others.

One tower was now wrapped in flames. The Black Knight's men ran through the castle wiping out the last of the enemy. Cedric rushed to find Rowena. Gurth ran at his heels. At last they found her room. They beat down the door. Gurth carried her to safety. Cedric went on, hunting Athelstane.

But Athelstane was already free. He and Wamba had broken out when the fire started. They ran down the stairs to the castle yard.

Here in the yard was the Templar. He was mounted on his horse. Around him were the last of his men. He had lowered the drawbridge, but he could not get to it. He was cut off by Locksley's men. Brian and his men fought like lions. Rebecca was on horseback with one of Brian's Arabian slaves. Brian watched and guarded her like a hawk. He held his great shield over her. All the while he cut and slashed at his foes.

Athelstane saw him as he came down the stairs. He thought the woman was Rowena. He rushed forward. He picked up a battle ax.

"Turn, false Templar," he shouted.

"Dog!" said the Templar, grinding his teeth. He rose in his stirrups. Down flew his mighty sword. Athelstane fell to the ground.

Now the Templar saw his chance.

"Follow me!" he cried. He dashed for the raft. He thundered over it, his men following.

"DeBracy! DeBracy!" he called. "Are you here?"

"I am here," answered DeBracy from the tower. "I am a prisoner."

"Can I save you?"

"No. I have given up. Save yourself. Get out of here. The Lion is loose. Get out of England."

The Templar and his men rode off in a cloud of dust.

One tower after another began to crash to earth. The great castle of Front-de-Boeuf was soon a ruin. Hardly a Norman was left.

Chapter XXV

LOCKSLEY'S outlaws gathered in the forest the day after the battle. Locksley was going to give each man a fair share of the things taken from the castle. There was a lot of silver, rich armor, and fine clothes.

Locksley sat down under a great oak tree. He told the Black Knight to sit at his right. He put Cedric at his left.

"I'm not trying to boss you," he said. "But I am king in these forests. Let's get on with this. Everybody will hear about the battle. We'd better be out of here. Cedric, first you take what you want for your Saxons."

"Give it all to your men. I can pay my men myself, Locksley," said Cedric. "All except Wamba. I can never pay him back. He was ready to die for me. Wamba stayed with me." Cedric put his arm around the clown.

"Master, you can do me a favor," said Wamba. "Name it."

"You can pardon my friend Gurth. He ran away, but only to help your son."

"Pardon him! I'll do more than that. Gurth, you are no longer a slave. I give you your freedom."

Gurth jumped for joy.

"Ho!" he cried. "Get me a file. Off comes this brass collar. I thank you, master."

Now they heard the tramp of horses. The Lady Rowena and her men came riding up. She had come to thank Locksley.

"God bless you brave men," she said. "If any of you are ever hungry, Rowena has food. If ever the Normans drive you away, live in my forests. I'll never ask how many deer you shoot."

"Thanks, gentle lady," said Locksley. "We were glad to help you."

Cedric got ready to go with her. He tried to get the Black Knight to go along.

"I know you knights like to fight," he said. "But you ought to have a home. Let Rotherwood be your home. Come and live there as my son or brother."

"I will come soon, my friend," said the Black Knight. "Now I have other things to do. I'm going to ask you a favor."

"You shall have it," said Cedric.

Now Locksley spoke to the Black Knight.

"Brave knight, take whatever you want."

"I want only one thing. I want you to turn over Sir Maurice DeBracy to me."

"He's yours," said Locksley.

"DeBracy," said the Black Knight, "you are free. Go. Don't ever let me see you again. Maurice DeBracy, if I do, *beware!*"

DeBracy bowed and galloped off.

"Noble knight," said Locksley, "take my bugle. Keep it to remember your outlaw friends. If ever you need us, blow this bugle three times. My outlaws will hear it and come."

"Thank you, Locksley," said the Black Knight. "I take it gladly."

"Men," said Locksley, "when you hear that bugle, you'll know the Black Knight wants you."

"Long live Locksley! Long live the Black Knight!" shouted the outlaws.

Now Locksley gave each man his share. As they finished, an outlaw came in with Isaac of York. A few minutes later two more came in. These two brought in Prior Aymer of Jorvaulx.

"Well," said the Prior angrily, "I guess you want ransom. How much?"

"Say," said an outlaw, "I've got an idea. Let's let the Jew set the Prior's ransom. Then the Prior can set the Jew's ransom. That's fair, isn't it?"

"Good!" said Locksley. "Here, Jew. Step up here.

Look at that holy Father Aymer. You know how much money he has. How much ransom should he pay?"

"Oh, yes," said Isaac. "I've done business with him before. He's rich. They've got plenty."

"Liar!" cried the Prior. "You know we've spent our money on our buildings. You Christian men shouldn't listen to him."

"Come on, Isaac," said Locksley. "How much?"

"Six hundred gold pieces," said Isaac. "He'll have plenty left—plenty."

"All right," said Locksley. "Six hundred it is."

"I can lend the money to him," said Isaac. "Then he can pay me back."

"Fine," said Locksley. "You can pay his and yours."

"Mine!" screamed Isaac. "I am a poor broken man! I have nothing. Fifty gold pieces would break me."

"The Prior will set your ransom," said Locksley. "How much, Prior? How much shall the Jew pay?"

"Isaac? He's rich! He's Isaac of York. He could ransom a king. One thousand gold pieces at least!"

"One thousand it is," said Locksley.

"The god of my fathers help me!" cried Isaac. "My daughter is gone, too. Oh, Rebecca! Where are you, where are you?"

"Does your daughter have black hair?" asked the outlaw. "And did she wear a black veil with a silver border?"

"She did! She did! Blessings on you! Where is she?"

"The Templar carried her off."

"Alas! My daughter! My daughter!"

"Friends," said Locksley, "the old man makes me feel sorry for him. Isaac, you'll need your money to ransom your daughter. We'll take only five hundred from you. Brian de Bois-Guilbert is at a Templars' house not far from here. You'd better get over there fast. Prior Aymer, you are a friend of Brian de Bois-Guilbert. Isaac will put up your ransom money. You can ask Brian to let Rebecca go for a ransom."

The Prior wrote a note. He handed it to Isaac. "This will help," he said.

Isaac and two outlaws started out. The Black Knight now got ready to leave, too. He mounted his big war horse and galloped off.

Chapter XXVI

WHILE this was going on, Prince John and the Norman nobles met at York. John wanted them to make him king of England. Waldemar Fitzurse did his best to help. Waldemar went from one noble to another. He told them Richard liked the Saxons. He told them John was their friend. But John and Waldemar were worried. Where was Front-de-Boeuf? Where were DeBracy and Brian? They needed those three bold men.

"Those villains!" said Prince John. "When I need them they are gone."

"They're not villains," said Waldemar. "They're fools. Chasing after those women! When we could be taking the country."

"What can we do?"

"I've told DeBracy's men to get ready. I'm going to send them to Front-de-Boeuf's castle."

"But who is this? Here comes DeBracy himself."

It was DeBracy. His armor was broken and dusty.

He was smeared with blood from head to foot. He pulled off his helmet.

"DeBracy," said Prince John, "what does this mean? Speak!"

"Speak, DeBracy," cried Fitzurse. "Where is the Templar? Where is Front-de-Boeuf?"

"The Templar got away. Front-de-Boeuf is dead. He's buried under the fire of his own castle. Only I am left."

"A fire, you say?"

"That's not the worst," said DeBracy. "Richard is in England. I saw him. I spoke to him."

Prince John turned pale. He held on to a chair. His knees shook.

"DeBracy!" said Fitzurse. "It can't be!"

"I was his prisoner," said DeBracy. "I spoke to him."

"With Richard Plantagenet?"

"With Richard Plantagenet. With Richard the Lion Hearted. With Richard, king of England."

"Has he an army?"

"Only a few outlaws. They don't know who he is. He joined them to storm Front-de-Boeuf's castle."

"What are you going to do, DeBracy?"

"I'm taking my men and getting out of England."

Prince John hung his head.

"They run away. I thought you fellows were

smart. I thought you had some nerve. You could win riches and honor. You run like rats."

"What can you do?" asked DeBracy. "When the people hear Richard is back, they'll join his army. That's the end of us. You'd better head for France yourself—and fast!"

"I'm not worried about myself," said John. "But I wouldn't like to see your heads hanging from a wall."

Waldemar and DeBracy looked at each other.

"There is one way out," said Prince John. "Richard is riding alone. If he is gone, we are safe."

"I won't touch him," said DeBracy quickly. "I was his prisoner. He spared my life. I'll do him no harm."

"Who said harm him?" laughed John. "No, a prison would be as good—in England or Austria. What's the difference?"

Chapter XXVII

BRIAN was at a Templar castle called Templestowe. The outlaws took Isaac to the gate and left him. He knocked.

In the castle yard walked a tall old white haired man. It was Lucas Beaumanoir, the Grand Master of all Templars. He had just come to England.

"A Jew is at the gate, noble Grand Master," said Conrad, the castle chief. "He asks to see Brother Brian de Bois-Guilbert."

"Bring the Jew in," commanded the Grand Master.

Conrad took Prior Aymer's letter from the Jew's shaking hand. The Grand Master read it.

"What is this, Conrad? Read it. And you, Jew, listen!"

Isaac heard these words:

"Dear Brother Brian:

I have been caught by Locksley's outlaws. They want ransom money. I hear you have got away with that beautiful Jewish witch, Rebecca.

115

Be careful. I hear your Grand Master is on the way to England. You know he does not care for cherry cheeks and black eyes. He will soon spoil your little game with Rebecca. So, watch yourself.

Your friend, *Prior Aymer.*"

"Ha! What about this, Conrad?" said the Grand Master. "Who is this witch?"

"He doesn't mean she's really a witch, Master. He means she's very beautiful."

"Nonsense, Conrad. This Rebecca of York was a pupil of the famous Jewess Miriam. We burned Miriam at the stake. She was a witch. Just watch."

The Grand Master turned to Isaac.

"Is your daughter a prisoner of Brian de Bois-Guilbert?"

"Yes, noble Master. I will pay—"

"Quiet! Your daughter has healed people, has she not?"

"Oh, yes, sir. She heals people the doctors cannot help."

The Grand Master smiled at Conrad. "See, Brother," he said. "She says magic words of the Devil, does she not?"

"Oh, no, sir. She has a secret medicine. She learned about it from Miriam, a Jewess."

"Liar!" screamed the Grand Master. "We burned

116

Miriam at the stake. Now we have her pupil. This Rebecca has bewitched our Brother Brian. He is out of his head. Throw this Jew out! Kill him if he comes back!"

A little later Rebecca heard footsteps. Conrad opened the door.

"Cursed Jewess," said he, "come, follow me."

"Where?"

"Girl, don't ask questions. Obey. You go to trial before our Grand Master."

"Gladly," said Rebecca. "I have nothing to fear."

They went down the stairs and into a great hall. The hall was filled with people. Conrad led her to her seat. As she passed through the crowd someone slipped a note into her hand.

On a high seat sat the Grand Master. He had on a long white robe. The front seats were filled with Templar priests. Back of them sat the Templar knights. Behind them sat the common people. All were eager to hear the trial of the Jewish witch.

Brian stood at one side, his eyes on the floor.

"See," whispered the Grand Master, "he cannot look at us. She has him under a magic spell. That's what the Devil can do!"

The Grand Master called in some witnesses. They told how Brian had fought to save Rebecca at the castle. Then a poor man was called in. Rebecca

117

had healed him when no one else could. Two other men told their stories. One had seen her use the medicine on Ivanhoe. The other one said he had seen Rebecca change herself into a swan. She had flown from the castle. Then she had come back and become a woman again. It was hard to tell if he really believed his own story. The Grand Master was ready to believe anything against her. At last they gave Rebecca a chance to talk.

"Yes," she said simply. "I have healed the wounded and sick. I use medicine—nothing else. I know nothing of the Devil. Ask your own Templar Knight. Ask Brian de Bois-Guilbert. He will tell you I have done nothing wrong."

Everyone looked at Brian. He looked at Rebecca.

"The note," he said.

Nobody knew what he meant except Rebecca. She took a quick look at the note in her hand. The note said, "Ask for a champion!"

Rebecca understood. People on trial could ask for a knight to fight for them. The judge picked another knight for the court. The two knights would fight. If the court knight won, the person was guilty. If the other knight won, the person went free. Brian wanted her to ask for a champion. He wanted her to pick him. He would fight and win. Then she would be free.

"Rebecca," said the Grand Master, "Brian will say nothing for you."

"There is a chance left for me," said Rebecca. "I ask for a champion."

"Ha!" laughed the Grand Master. "Who will fight for a Jewish witch?"

"God will send me a champion," said Rebecca.

"All right," said the Grand Master. "We will leave it in God's hands. Brothers, who shall fight for the Templars?"

"Brian de Bois-Guilbert," said Conrad.

"Good," said the Grand Master. "Brian de Bois-Guilbert it shall be. Rebecca, you have three days to get a champion. The trial is over."

Rebecca was led back to her room. A few minutes later she heard a soft knock on the door.

"Come in," she called.

Brian came in.

"Do not be afraid of me, Rebecca," he said.

"You got me into this," she answered.

"Rebecca, I couldn't help it. I didn't know they would pick me to fight for them. I was going to fight as your champion. You would have been free. I would do anything for you."

"Then go to King Richard for help."

"Never!"

"Then good-bye."

"I wish I had never met you, Rebecca. Or, I wish you were a Christian. Forgive me, Rebecca, will you?"

"I do forgive you."

"Good-bye, then," said Brian. He walked out and closed the door behind him.

Chapter XXVIII

WHEN the Black Knight left Locksley, he rode straight to the St. Botolph Abbey. Wamba and Gurth had brought the wounded Ivanhoe here.

"Wilfred," said the Black Knight, "I will meet you at Rotherwood. I want to talk to your father. I'm going to see that you and Cedric stop your foolish quarreling. I've got to go now. I'm taking Wamba to show me the way."

"Why can't I go with you?"

"You're not quite healed yet. You need another day's rest. Good-bye, Wilfred."

Wilfred kissed his hand. The Black Knight and Wamba rode off into the forest.

That evening Wilfred felt much better. He put on his armor and called for his horse. Soon he and Gurth were following the Black Knight's trail.

The Black Knight and Wamba were riding along talking about the outlaws. Wamba's sharp eyes were looking ahead.

"What would you do, Sir Knight, if we met two forest robbers?" he asked.

"Pin them down with my lance if they troubled us," said the Black Knight.

"What if there were four?"

"Same thing."

"How about six? Wouldn't you blow Locksley's bugle for help?"

"No! Not for twenty."

"May I look at the bugle?"

The knight handed Wamba the bugle. Wamba hung it around his own neck.

"Now look at those trees over there. Somebody is lying in wait for us."

"Wamba, you're right!"

As he spoke, three arrows hit his armor. The Black Knight spurred his horse and charged. Six or seven men rode out to meet him. Three lances hit him and splintered like wood. The Black Knight pulled out his sword and began swinging. His enemies began to go down with each mighty blow.

121

A knight in blue armor now charged from the side. He aimed his lance at the Black Knight's horse. Down went the horse, taking the Black Knight with him.

Now Wamba had a chance to blow the bugle. He blew three times. Then he ran in and helped the Black Knight get loose from the horse.

"Come, you coward," called the knight in blue armor. "Let's get him."

The Black Knight now backed against an oak tree and fought with his sword. The knight in blue armor held back. When he saw his chance, he rode forward. He tried to pin the Black Knight against the tree with his lance. But Wamba skipped in quickly. He slashed the knight's horse through the hind leg. Down went man and horse.

Five or six men were now after the Black Knight. As they closed in, the first man suddenly fell. An arrow was sticking in his back. A moment later Locksley and a dozen men burst out of the forest. They ended the fight in a hurry.

"Thank you again, my friend," said the Black Knight. "Wamba, pull off that helmet. I want to see who this blue knight is."

Wamba loosened the helmet.

"Waldemar Fitzurse!" said the Black Knight.

"Yes, Richard," said Fitzurse.

"Who sent you to do this, Waldemar?"

"Your brother John."

"All right. Get out. I'll give you three days. Get out of England. Never tell anybody that my brother had you do this. Locksley, let him have a horse."

Locksley did.

"I'd like to plant an arrow in his back," said Locksley. "But you're the boss."

"Yes," said the Black Knight. "I am, Locksley. I am Richard the Lion Hearted, king of England."

The outlaws stared a minute. Then they dropped to their knees.

"Rise, my friends," he said kindly. "And you, Locksley—"

"Don't call me Locksley. I'll tell you my real name, too. I guess you've heard of me. I am Robin Hood of Sherwood Forest."

"King of outlaws, and prince of good fellows!" said the King. "You will always be my friend and I will be yours."

Chapter XXIX

ILFRED and Gurth now caught up with Richard and Wamba. The four rode on together to Rotherwood. Robin Hood and his men went back to their forests.

Cedric was glad to see the Black Knight. Richard told Wilfred to keep his helmet on. He did not want Cedric to know his son was there. He went down to talk to Cedric. Wilfred followed him down the stairs.

"Cedric," said Richard, "you said you'd do me a favor. Do you remember?"

"I do. I will. Ask what you want. You shall have it."

"First, I want to tell you something. You know me as the Black Knight. Cedric, I am Richard Plantagenet, king of England."

"What! Richard the Lion Hearted?"

"Yes, Cedric. I know you Saxons do not like the Normans. I am part Saxon and part Norman. But I am not king of Normans or of Saxons. I am king of England. We must live together in peace. Saxons will have their rights."

"We Saxons look upon you as our king. You are the noblest of all the Normans." Cedric dropped to his knee and kissed Richard's hand.

"Now, Cedric, about that favor. I want you to forgive your son Wilfred. He is my friend. He is a good son."

Wilfred came forward. He knelt down before his father.

"My father," he said, "let us forget our quarrel."

"I forgive you, my son," said Cedric. He raised Wilfred to his feet. "But about Rowena—"

Just then Athelstane came in.

"Father Cedric," said Athelstane, "be sensible about Rowena. The lady does not care for me. I know it. She loves Wilfred's little finger more than all of me. She—ah, but here she comes herself."

Athelstane took Rowena's hand. Then he took Wilfred's hand. He put Rowena's hand into Wilfred's.

"There," he said, "now that's settled."

Gurth now looked into the room. He gave Wilfred a signal. Wilfred followed him out. A few minutes later Richard went to look for him. Ivanhoe was gone. Gurth was gone. At last Richard found a servant who had seen them.

"A Jew came with a letter, Sir Knight. He asked for Wilfred of Ivanhoe. Wilfred spoke to him. Then he called for his horse and armor. Gurth went with him. They rushed from the castle."

"Send the Jew to me quickly," said Richard.

When he came, Richard talked with him.

"Armor!" he roared. "Bring me my horse and armor!"

Soon Richard was thundering over the drawbridge and down the road in a cloud of dust.

Chapter XXX

REBECCA'S three days were up. Crowds were pouring into Templestowe Castle. The castle yard was ready. Seats were built around the sides. At the east end was the Grand Master's throne. Around the throne were seats for the Templar priests and knights. At the other end of the yard stood the wooden stake. It was driven deep into the ground. There Rebeca was to be tied and burned alive. Wood lay piled high around the stake. Behind the stake four black slaves stood ready.

The heavy church bell began to ring. The great drawbridge came down, and the gates swung open. Out rode six squires with trumpets. Behind them came a knight carrying the Templar banner. Next came a band of Templar knights. Then the Grand Master came, riding on a white horse. After him rode Brian de Bois-Guilbert. Brian wore a shining suit of armor. He was pale as death. He handled his plunging horse easily, though.

Behind Brian rode more Templar knights, pages and squires, dressed in black. Now, in the center of a guard, came Rebecca. A long coarse white robe covered her from neck to foot.

The guards led Rebecca to a black chair near the stake. She shivered a little and moved her lips in prayer.

The Grand Master sat down on his throne. Conrad stepped before the throne.

"Noble Grand Master!" he cried. "Here stands the good knight Brian de Bois-Guilbert. He is ready to fight. He will prove this woman Rebecca is a witch working with the devil."

The trumpets blew. A herald stepped forward.

"Hear you! Hear you!" he called. "Here stands Brian de Bois-Guilbert ready to do battle. Any champion may now come forward to fight for Rebecca, the Jewish witch."

The trumpets sounded again. All was quiet for many minutes.

"No champion comes," said the Grand Master. "Go ask Rebecca if someone will fight for her."

"Tell the Grand Master I have done nothing wrong. I want as much time as I can have. I hope God will send me a champion."

The herald told the Grand Master what she had said.

"She shall have time. We wait until the shadows point east. Then she must die."

Brian stood near Rebecca.

"Rebecca," he called softly, "can you hear me?"

"I don't want to hear you."

"Rebecca, listen! We've got a chance! Get up here behind me. We can make a run for it."

"I'll not go with *you*," answered Rebecca.

Now Conrad came forward.

"The shadows point east. Rebecca, get ready to die."

But at this moment a hundred voices cried out, "A champion! A champion!"

A lone knight came riding toward the castle. But as he came closer, hope died. His horse was so tired he staggered. The knight could hardly hold himself in the saddle. The herald asked him his name and what he wanted.

129

"I am here to fight for Rebecca, daughter of Isaac of York. I will prove she has done no wrong. I call Brian de Bois-Guilbert a traitor, murderer, and liar! May God, Our Lady, and St. George help me! I am Wilfred of Ivanhoe."

"I will not fight you now," said the Templar. "First get your wound healed. Get a fresh horse. Then I'll fight you. You haven't got a chance."

"Ha, proud Templar! Have you forgotten? I've beaten you twice. Are you afraid?"

"Saxon dog! Take your lance. Die if you must."

"Rebecca," said Ivanhoe, "do you take me for your champion?"

"I do!" cried Rebecca. "But I'm afraid! You are wounded. I don't want you to die."

Ivanhoe was already at his place. Bois-Guilbert took his. His squire looked at him in surprise. Brian's pale white face was flushed and red. He looked sick.

The Grand Master called, "Let go!" The trumpets blew.

The knights charged. The Templar's lance hit Ivanhoe's shield. Ivanhoe's lance crashed into Brian's shield. Ivanhoe's tired horse went down. The Templar was not hit hard enough to go down, but to everyone's surprise, Brian fell.

Ivanhoe climbed to his feet. His sword was out.

He ran toward Brian. But Brian did not rise. Wilfred put his foot on the Templar's chest. He put his sword to Brian's throat.

"Give up or die!" he cried. Brian did not answer.

"Do not kill him!" cried the Grand Master. "He is beaten. The girl goes free."

They took off Brian's helmet. His eyes were closed. The flush had died from his face. It was pale as death. It was death. Brian de Bois-Guilbert had been dead before he fell.

"This is God's will," said the Grand Master. "His will be done."

Chapter XXXI

KING RICHARD got there as they carried Brian away.

"I am too late, I see," said he. "I wanted to fight him myself. Men, do your duty."

A knight stepped forward. He laid his hand on Conrad's shoulder.

"I arrest you—" he began.

"Who dares arrest a Templar Knight?" cried the Grand Master.

"I do," said Richard. "I, Richard Plantagenet, have him arrested. The Templars have plotted against me. The Templars are through in England."

The Grand Master stormed. But before the sun went down he led a long line of Templars from the castle. The flag of England flew from the castle towers.

"What is the news from York?" asked Ivanhoe.

"The Norman nobles have scattered," answered a knight. "Prince John has gone to France. Richard Plantagenet rules in England."

Not long after, Wilfred of Ivanhoe and Rowena were married. Richard himself was at the wedding. Ivanhoe and Cedric were Richard's trusted friends until his death.

Rebecca and Isaac of York left England to live in Spain. Rebecca spent her life healing the sick and wounded and helping the poor. She never married. Too often her mind went back to the gallant knight who risked his life to save hers—Wilfred of Ivanhoe.